Mother

Kathleen Norris

Mother

MOTHER

Published in the United States by IndyPublish.com
Boston, Massachusetts

ISBN 1-4219-2320-3 (hardcover)

TO

J. E. T. AND J. A. T. As years ago we carried to your knees The tales and treasures of eventful days, Knowing no deed too humble for your praise, Nor any gift too trivial to please, So still we bring, with older smiles and tears, What gifts we may, to claim the old, dear right; Your faith, beyond the silence and the night, Your love still close and watching through the years.

CHAPTER I

"Well, we couldn't have much worse weather than this for the last week of school, could we?" Margaret Paget said in discouragement. She stood at one of the school windows, her hands thrust deep in her coat pockets for warmth, her eyes following the whirling course of the storm that howled outside. The day had commenced with snow, but now, at twelve o'clock, the rain was falling in sheets, and the barren schoolhouse yard, and the play-shed roof, ran muddy streams of water.

Margaret had taught in this schoolroom for nearly four years now, ever since her seventeenth birthday, and she knew every feature of the big bare room by heart, and every detail of the length of village street that the high, uncurtained windows commanded. She had stood at this window in all weathers: when locust and lilac made even ugly little Weston enchanting, and all the windows were open to floods of sweet spring air; when tie dry heat of autumn burned over the world; when the common little houses and barns, and the bare trees, lay dazzling and transfigured under the first snowfall, and the wood crackled in the schoolroom stove; and when, as to-day, midwinter rains swept drearily past the windows, and the children must have the lights lighted for their writing lesson. She was tired of it all, with an utter and hopeless weariness. Tired of the bells, and the whispering, and the shuffling feet, of the books that smelled of pencil-dust and ink and little dusty fingers; tired of the blackboards, cleaned in great irregular scallops by small and zealous arms; of the clear-ticking big clock; of little girls who sulked, and little girls who cried after hours in the hall because they had lost their lunch baskets or their over-shoes, and little girls who had colds in their heads, and no handker-chiefs. Looking out into the gray day and the rain, Margaret said to herself that she was sick of it all!

There were no little girls in the schoolroom now. They were for the most part downstairs in the big playroom, discussing cold lunches, and planning, presumably, the joys of the closely approaching holi-days. One or two windows had been partially opened to air the room in their absence, and Margaret's only companion was another teacher, Emily Porter, a cheerful little widow, whose plain rosy face was in marked contrast to the younger woman's unusual beauty.

Mrs. Porter loved Margaret and admired her very much, but she her-self loved teaching. She had had a hard fight to secure this position a few years ago; it meant comfort to her and her children, and it still seemed to her a miracle of God's working, after her years of struggle and worry. She could not understand why Margaret wanted anything better; what better thing indeed could life hold! Sometimes, looking admiringly at her associate's crown of tawny braids, at the dark eyes and the exquisite lines of mouth and forehead, Mrs. Porter would find herself sympathetic with the girl's vague discontent and long-ings, to the extent of wishing that some larger social circle than that of Weston might have a chance to appreciate Margaret Paget's beau-ty, that "some of those painters who go crazy over girls not half as pretty" might see her. But after all, sensible little Mrs. Porter would say to herself, Weston was a "nice" town, only four hours from New York, absolutely up-to-date; and Weston's best people were all "nice," and the Paget girls were very popular, and "went everywhere," — young people were just discontented and exacting, that was all!

She came to Margaret's side now, buttoned snugly into her own storm coat, and they looked out at the rain together. Nothing alive was in sight. The bare trees tossed in the wind, and a garden gate halfway down the row of little shabby cottages banged and banged.

"Shame—this is the worst yet!" Mrs. Porter said. "You aren't going home to lunch in all this, Margaret?"

"Oh, I don't know," Margaret said despondently. "I'm so dead that I'd make a cup of tea here if I didn't think Mother would worry and send Julie over with lunch."

"I brought some bread and butter—but not much. I hoped it would hold up. I hate to leave Tom and Sister alone all day," Mrs. Porter said dubiously. "There's tea and some of those bouillon cubes and some crackers left. But you're so tired, I don't know but what you ought to have a hearty lunch."

"Oh, I'm not hungry." Margaret dropped into a desk, put her elbows on it, pushed her hair off her forehead. The other woman saw a tear slip by the lowered, long lashes.

"You're exhausted, aren't you, Margaret?" she said suddenly.

The little tenderness was too much. Margaret's lip shook.

"Dead!" she said unsteadily. Presently she added, with an effort at cheerfulness, "I'm just cross, I guess, Emily; don't mind me! I'm tired out with examinations and—" her eyes filled again—"and I'm sick of wet cold weather and rain and snow," she added childishly. "Our house is full of muddy rubbers and wet clothes! Other people go places and do pleasant things," said Margaret, her breast rising and falling stormily; "but nothing ever happens to us except broken arms, and bills, and boilers bursting, and chicken-pox! It's drudge, drudge, drudge, from morning until night!"

With a sudden little gesture of abandonment she found a handkerchief in her belt, and pressed it, still folded, against her eyes. Mrs. Porter watched her solicitously, but silently. Outside the schoolroom windows the wind battered furiously, and rain slapped steadily against the panes.

"Well!" the girl said resolutely and suddenly. And after a moment she added frankly, "I think the real trouble to-day, Emily, is that we just heard of Betty Forsythe's engagement—she was my brother's girl, you know; he's admired her ever since she got into High School, and of course Bruce is going to feel awfully bad."

"Betty engaged? Who to?" Mrs. Porter was interested.

"To that man—boy, rather, he's only twenty-one—who's been visiting the Redmans," Margaret said. "She's only known him two weeks."

"Gracious! And she's only eighteen—"

"Not quite eighteen. She and my sister, Julie, were in my first class four years ago; they're the same age," Margaret said. "She came fluttering over to tell us last night, wearing a diamond the size of a marble! Of course,"—Margaret was loyal,—"I don't think there's a jealous bone in Julie's body; still, it's pretty hard! Here's Julie plugging away to get through the Normal School, so that she can teach all the rest of her life, and Betty's been to California, and been to Europe, and now is going to marry a rich New York man! Betty's the only child, you know, so, of course, she has everything. It seems so unfair, for Mr. Forsythe's salary is exactly what Dad's is; yet they can travel, and keep two maids, and entertain all the time! And as for family, why, Mother's family is one of the finest in the country, and Dad's had two uncles who were judges—and what were the Forsythes! However,"—Margaret dried her eyes and put away her handkerchief,—"however, it's for Bruce I mind most!"

"Bruce is only three years older than you are, twenty-three or four," Mrs. Porter smiled.

"Yes, but he's not the kind that forgets!" Margaret's flush was a little resentful. "Oh, of course, you can laugh, Emily. I know that there are plenty of people who don't mind dragging along day after day, working and eating and sleeping—but I'm not that kind!" she went on moodily. "I used to hope that things would be different; it makes me sick to think how brave I was; but now here's Ju coming along, and Ted growing up, and Bruce's girl throwing him over—it's all so unfair! I look at the Cutter girls, nearly fifty, and running the post-office for thirty years, and Mary Page in the Library, and the Norberrys painting pillows,—and I could scream!"

"Things will take a turn for the better some day, Margaret," said the other woman, soothingly; "and as time goes on you'll find yourself getting more and more pleasure out of your work, as I do. Why, I've never been so securely happy in my life as I am now. You'll feel differently some day."

"Maybe," Margaret assented unenthusiastically. There was a pause. Perhaps the girl was thinking that to teach school, live in a plain little cottage on the unfashionable Bridge Road, take two roomers, and cook and sew and plan for Tom and little Emily, as Mrs. Porter did, was not quite an ideal existence.

"You're an angel, anyway, Emily," said she, affectionately, a little shamefacedly. "Don't mind my growling. I don't do it very often. But I look about at other people, and then realize how my mother's slaved for twenty years and how my father's been tied down, and I've come to the conclusion that while there may have been a time when a woman could keep a house, tend a garden, sew and spin and raise twelve children, things are different now; life is more complicated. You owe your husband something, you owe yourself something. I want to get on, to study and travel, to be a companion to my husband. I don't want to be a mere upper servant!"

"No, of course not," assented Mrs. Porter, vaguely, soothingly.

"Well, if we are going to stay here, I'll light the stove," Margaret said after a pause. "B-r-r-r! this room gets cold with the windows open! I wonder why Kelly doesn't bring us more wood?"

"I guess—I'll stay!" Mrs. Porter said uncertainly, following her to the big book closet off the schoolroom, where a little gas stove and a small china closet occupied one wide shelf. The water for the tea and bouillon was put over the flame in a tiny enamelled saucepan; they set forth on a fringed napkin crackers and sugar and spoons.

At this point, a small girl of eleven with a brilliant, tawny head, and a wide and toothless smile, opened the door cautiously, and said, blinking rapidly with excitement,—

"Mark, Mother theth pleath may thee come in?"

This was Rebecca, one of Margaret's five younger brothers and sisters, and a pupil of the school herself. Margaret smiled at the eager little face.

"Hello, darling! Is Mother here? Certainly she can! I believe,"—she said, turning, suddenly radiant, to Mrs. Porter,—"I'll just bet you she's brought us some lunch!"

"Thee brought uth our luncheth—eggth and thpith caketh and everything!" exulted Rebecca, vanishing, and a moment later Mrs. Paget appeared.

She was a tall woman, slender but large of build, and showing, under a shabby raincoat and well pinned-up skirt, the gracious generous lines of shoulders and hips, the deep-bosomed erect figure that is rarely seen except in old daguerreotypes, or the ideal of some artist two generations ago. The storm to-day had blown an unusual color into her thin cheeks, her bright, deep eyes were like Margaret's, but the hair that once had shown an equally golden lustre was dull and smooth now, and touched with gray. She came in smiling, and a little breathless,

"Mother, you didn't come out in all this rain just to bring us our lunches!" Margaret protested, kissing the cold, fresh face.

"Well, look at the lunch you silly girls were going to eat!" Mrs. Paget protested in turn, in a voice rich with amusement. "I love to walk in the rain, Mark; I used to love it when I was a girl. Tom and Sister are at our house, Mrs. Potter, playing with Duncan and Baby. I'll keep them until after school, then I'll send them over to walk home with you."

"Oh, you are an angel!" said the younger mother, gratefully. And "You are an angel, Mother!" Margaret echoed, as Mrs. Paget opened a shabby suitcase, and took from it a large jar of hot rich soup, a little blue bowl of stuffed eggs, half a fragrant whole-wheat loaf in a white napkin, a little glass full of sweet butter, and some of the spice cakes to which Rebecca had already enthusiastically alluded.

"There!" said she, pleased with their delight, "now take your time, you've got three-quarters of an hour. Julie devilled the eggs, and the sweet-butter man happened to come just as I was starting."

"Delicious!—You've saved our lives," Margaret said, busy with cups and spoons. "You'll stay, Mother?" she broke off suddenly, as Mrs. Paget closed the suitcase.

"I can't, dear! I must go back to the children," her mother said cheerfully. No coaxing proving of any avail, Margaret went with her to the top of the hall stairs.

"What's my girl worrying about?" Mrs. Paget asked, with a keen glance at Margaret's face.

"Oh, nothing!" Margaret used both hands to button the top button of her mother's coat. "I was hungry and cold, and I didn't want to walk home in the rain!" she confessed, raising her eyes to the eyes so near her own.

"Well, go back to your lunch," Mrs. Paget urged, after a brief pause, not quite satisfied with the explanation. Margaret kissed her again, watched her descend the stairs, and leaning over the banister called down to her softly:

"Don't worry about me, Mother!"

"No—no—no!" her mother called back brightly. Indeed, Margaret reflected, going back to the much-cheered Emily, it was not in her nature to worry.

No, Mother never worried, or if she did, nobody ever knew it. Care, fatigue, responsibility, hard long years of busy days and broken nights had left their mark on her face; the old beauty that had been hers was chiselled to a mere pure outline now; but there was a contagious serenity in Mrs. Paget's smile, a clear steadiness in her calm eyes, and her forehead, beneath an unfashionably plain sweep of hair, was untroubled and smooth.

The children's mother was a simple woman; so absorbed in the hourly problems attendant upon the housing and feeding of her husband and family that her own personal ambitions, if she had any, were quite lost sight of, and the actual outlines of her character were forgotten by every one, herself included. If her busy day marched successfully to nightfall; if darkness found her husband reading in his big chair, the younger children sprawled safe and asleep in the shabby nursery, the older ones contented with books or games, the clothes sprinkled, the bread set, the kitchen dark and clean; Mrs. Paget asked no more of life. She would sit, her overflowing work-basket beside her, looking from one absorbed face to another, thinking perhaps of Julie's new school dress, of Ted's impending siege with the dentist, or of the old bureau up attic that might be mended for Bruce's room. "Thank God we have all warm beds," she would say, when they all went upstairs, yawning and chilly.

She had married, at twenty, the man she loved, and had found him better than her dreams in many ways, and perhaps disappointing in some few others, but "the best man in the world" for all that. That for more than twenty years he had been satisfied to stand for nine hours daily behind one dingy desk, and to carry home to her his unopened salary envelope twice a month, she found only admirable. Daddy was "steady," he was "so gentle with the children," he was "the easiest man in the world to cook for." "Bless his heart, no woman ever had less to worry over in her husband!" she would say, looking from her kitchen window to the garden where he trained the pea-vines, with the children's yellow heads bobbing about him. She never analyzed his character, much less criticised him. Good and bad, he was taken for granted; she was much more lenient to him than to any of the children. She welcomed the fast-coming babies as gifts from God, marvelled over their tiny perfectness, dreamed over the soft relaxed little forms with a heart almost too full for prayer. She was, in a word, old-fashioned, hopelessly out of the modern current of thoughts and events. She secretly regarded her children as marvel-

lous, even while she laughed down their youthful conceit and pun-
ished their naughtiness.

Thinking a little of all these things, as a girl with her own wifehood
and motherhood all before her does think, Margaret went back to her
hot luncheon. One o'clock found her at her desk, refreshed in spirit
by her little outburst, and much fortified in body. The room was well
aired, and a reinforced fire roared in the little stove. One of the children had brought her a spray of pine, and the spicy fragrance of it
reminded her that Christmas and the Christmas vacation were near;
her mind was pleasantly busy with anticipation of the play that the
Pagets always wrote and performed some time during the holidays,
and with the New Year's costume dance at the Hall, and a dozen less-
er festivities.

Suddenly, in the midst of a droning spelling lesson, there was a jar-
ring interruption. From the world outside came a child's shrill
screaming, which was instantly drowned in a chorus of frightened
voices, and in the schoolroom below her own Margaret heard a thun-
dering rush of feet, and answering screams. With a suffocating terror
at her heart she ran to the window, followed by every child in the
room.

The rain had stopped now, and the sky showed a pale, cold, yellow
light low in the west. At the schoolhouse gate an immense limousine
car had come to a stop. The driver, his face alone visible between a great
leather coat and visored leather cap, was talking unheard above the din.
A tall woman, completely enveloped in sealskins, had evidently
jumped from the limousine, and now held in her arms what made
Margaret's heart turn sick and cold, the limp figure of a small girl.

About these central figures there surged the terrified crying small
children of the just-dismissed primer class, and in the half moment
that Margaret watched, Mrs. Porter, white and shaking, and another
teacher, Ethel Elliot, an always excitable girl, who was now sobbing

and chattering hysterically, ran out from the school, each followed by her own class of crowding and excited boys and girls.

With one horrified exclamation, Margaret ran downstairs, and out to the gate. Mrs. Porter caught at her arm as she passed her in the path.

"Oh, my God, Margaret! It's poor little Dorothy Scott!" she said. "They've killed her. The car went completely over her!"

"Oh, Margaret, don't go near, oh, how can you!" screamed Miss Elliot. "Oh, and she's all they have! Who'll tell her mother!"

With astonishing ease, for the children gladly recognized authority, Margaret pushed through the group to the motor-car.

"Stop screaming—stop that shouting at once—keep still, every one of you!" she said angrily, shaking various shoulders as she went with such good effect that the voice of the woman in sealskins could be heard by the time Margaret reached her.

"I don't think she's badly hurt!" said this woman, nervously and eagerly. She was evidently badly shaken, and was very white. "Do quiet them, can't you?" she said, with a sort of apprehensive impatience. "Can't we take her somewhere, and get a doctor? Can't we get out of this?"

Margaret took the child in her own arms. Little Dorothy roared afresh, but to Margaret's unspeakable relief she twisted about and locked her arms tightly about the loved teacher's neck. The other woman watched them anxiously.

"That blood on her frock's just nosebleed," she said; "but I think the car went over her! I assure you we were running very slowly. How it happened—! But I don't think she was struck."

"Nosebleed!" Margaret echoed, with a great breath. "No," she said quietly, over the agitated little head; "I don't think she's much hurt. We'll take her in. Now, look here, children," she added loudly to the assembled pupils of the Weston Grammar School, whom mere curiosity had somewhat quieted, "I want every one of you children to go back to your schoolrooms; do you understand? Dorothy's had a bad scare, but she's got no bones broken, and we're going to have a doctor see that she's all right. I want you to see how quiet you can be. Mrs. Porter, may my class go into your room a little while?"

"Certainly," said Mrs. Porter, eager to cooperate, and much relieved to have her share of the episode take this form. "Form lines, children," she added calmly.

"Ted," said Margaret to her own small brother, who was one of Mrs. Porter's pupils, and who had edged closer to her than any boy unprivileged by relationship dared, "will you go down the street, and ask old Doctor Potts to come here? And then go tell Dorothy's mother that Dorothy has had a little bump, and that Miss Paget says she's all right, but that she'd like her mother to come for her."

"Sure I will, Mark!" Theodore responded enthusiastically, departing on a run.

"Mama!" sobbed the little sufferer at this point, hearing a familiar word.

" Yes, darling, you want Mama, don't you?" Margaret said soothingly, as she started with her burden up the schoolhouse steps. "What were you doing, Dorothy," she went on pleasantly, "to get under that big car?"

"I dropped my ball!" wailed the small girl, her tears beginning afresh, "and it rolled and rolled. And I didn't see the automobile, and I didn't see it! And I fell down and b-b-bumped my nose!"

"Well, I should think you did!" Margaret said, laughing. "Mother won't know you at all with such a muddy face and such a muddy apron!"

Dorothy laughed shakily at this, and several other little girls, passing in orderly file, laughed heartily. Margaret crossed the lines of children to the room where they played and ate their lunches on wet days. She shut herself in with the child and the fur-clad lady.

"Now you're all right!" said Margaret, gayly. And, Dorothy was presently comfortable in a big chair, wrapped in a rug from the motor-car, with her face washed, and her head dropped languidly back against her chair, as became an interesting invalid. The Irish janitor was facetious as he replenished the fire, and made her laugh again. Margaret gave her a numerical chart to play with, and saw with satisfaction that the little head was bent interestedly over it.

Quiet fell upon the school; the muffled sound of lessons recited in concert presently reached them. Theodore returned, reporting that the doctor would come as soon as he could and that Dorothy's mother was away at a card-party, but that Dorothy's "girl" would come for her as soon as the bread was out of the oven. There was nothing to do but wait.

"It seems a miracle," said the strange lady, in a low tone, when she and Margaret were alone again with the child. "But I don't believe she was scratched!"

"I don't think so," Margaret agreed. "Mother says no child who can cry is very badly hurt."

"They made such a horrible noise," said the other, sighing wearily. She passed a white hand, with one or two blazing great stones upon it, across her forehead. Margaret had leisure now to notice that by all signs this was a very great lady indeed. The quality of her furs, the glimpse of her gown that the loosened coat showed, her rings, and most of all the tones of her voice, the authority of her manner, the well-groomed hair and skin and hands, all marked the thoroughbred.

"Do you know that you managed that situation very cleverly just now?" said the lady, with a keen glance that made Margaret color. "One has such a dread of the crowd, just public sentiment, you know. Some odious bystander calls the police, they crowd against your driver, perhaps a brick gets thrown. We had an experience in England once—" She paused, then interrupted herself. "But I don't know your name?" she said brightly.

Margaret supplied it, was led to talk a little of her own people.

"Seven of you, eh? Seven's too many," said the visitor, with the assurance that Margaret was to learn characterized her. "I've two myself, two girls," she went on. "I wanted a boy, but they're nice girls. And you've six brothers and sisters? Are they all as handsome as you and this Teddy of yours? And why do you like teaching?"

"Why do I like it?" Margaret said, enjoying these confidences and the unusual experience of sitting idle in mid-afternoon. "I don't, I hate it."

"I see. But then why don't you come down to New York, and do something else?" the other woman asked.

"I'm needed at home, and I don't know any one there," Margaret said simply.

"I see," the lady said again thoughtfully. There was a pause. Then the same speaker said reminiscently, "I taught school once for three months when I was a girl, to show my father I could support myself."

"I've taught for four years," Margaret said.

"Well, if you ever want to try something else,—there are such lots of fascinating things a girl can do now!—be sure you come and see me about it," the stranger said. "I am Mrs. Carr-Boldt, of New York."

Margaret's amazed eyes flashed to Mrs. Carr-Boldt's face; her cheeks crimsoned.

"Mrs. Carr-Boldt!" she echoed blankly.

"Why not?" smiled the lady, not at all displeased.

"Why," stammered Margaret, laughing and rosy, "why, nothing— only I never dreamed who you were!" she finished, a little confused.

And indeed it never afterward seemed to her anything short of a miracle that brought the New York society woman—famed on two continents and from ocean to ocean for her jewels, her entertainments, her gowns, her establishments—into a Weston schoolroom, and into Margaret Paget's life.

"I was on my way to New York now," said Mrs. Carr-Boldt.

"I don't see why you should be delayed," Margaret said, glad to be able to speak normally, with such a fast-beating and pleasantly excited heart. "I'm sure Dorothy's all right."

"Oh, I'd rather wait. I like my company," said the other. And Margaret decided in that instant that there never was a more deservedly admired and copied and quoted woman.

Presently their chat was interrupted by the tramp of the departing school children; the other teachers peeped in, were reassured, and went their ways. Then came the doctor, to pronounce the entirely cheerful Dorothy unhurt, and to bestow upon her some hoarhound drops. Mrs. Carr-Boldt settled at once with the doctor, and when Margaret saw the size of the bill that was pressed into his hand, she realized that she had done her old friend a good turn.

"Use it up on your poor people," said Mrs. Carr-Boldt, to his protestations; and when he had gone, and Dorothy's "girl" appeared, she tipped that worthy and amazed Teuton, and after promising Dorothy a big doll from a New York shop, sent the child and maid home in the motor-car.

"I hope this hasn't upset your plans," Margaret said, as they stood waiting in the doorway. It was nearly five o'clock, the school was empty and silent.

"No, not exactly. I had hoped to get home for dinner. But I think I'll get Woolcock to take me back to Dayton; I've some very dear friends there who'll give me a cup of tea. Then I'll come back this way and get home, by ten, I should think, for a late supper." Then, as the limousine appeared, Mrs. Carr-Boldt took both Margaret's hands in hers, and said, "And now good-bye, my dear girl. I've got your address, and I'm going to send you something pretty to remember me by. You saved me from I don't know what annoyance and publicity. And don't forget that when you come to New York I'm going to help you meet the people you want to, and give you a start if I can. You're far too clever and good-looking to waste your life down here. Good-bye!"

"Good-bye!" Margaret said, her cheeks brilliant, her head awhirl.

She stood unmindful of the chilly evening air, watching the great motor-car wheel and slip into the gloom. The rain was over; a dying wind moaned mysteriously through the dusk. Margaret went slowly upstairs, pinned on her hat, buttoned her long coat snugly about her. She locked the schoolroom door, and, turning the corner, plunged her hands into her pockets, and faced the wind bravely. Deepening darkness and coldness were about her, but she felt surrounded by the warmth and brightness of her dreams. She saw the brilliant streets of a big city, the carriages and motor-cars coming and going, the idle, lovely women in their sumptuous gowns and hats. These things were real, near—almost attainable—to-night.

"Mrs. Carr-Boldt!" Margaret said, "the darling! I wonder if I'll ever see her again!"

CHAPTER II

Life in the shabby, commonplace house that sheltered the Paget family sometimes really did seem to proceed, as Margaret had suggested, in a long chain of violent shocks, narrow escapes, and closely averted catastrophes. No sooner was Duncan's rash pronounced not to be scarlet fever than Robert swallowed a penny, or Beck set fire to the dining-room waste-basket, or Dad foresaw the immediate failure of the Weston Home Savings Bank, and the inevitable loss of his position there. Sometimes there was a paternal explosion because Bruce liked to murmur vaguely of "dandy chances in Manila," or because Julie, pretty, excitable, and sixteen, had an occasional dose of stage fever, and would stammer desperately between convulsive sobs that she wasn't half as much afraid of "the terrible temptations of the life" as she was afraid of dying a poky old maid in Weston. In short, the home was crowded, the Pagets were poor, and every one of the seven possessed a spirited and distinct entity. All the mother's effort could not keep them always contented. Growing ambitions made the Weston horizon seem narrow and mean, and the young eyes that could not see beyond to-morrow were often wet with rebellious tears.

Through it all they loved each other; sometimes whole weeks went by in utter harmony; the children contented over "Parches" on the

hearthrug in the winter evenings, Julie singing in the morning sunlight, as she filled the vases from the shabby marguerite bushes on the
lawn. But there were other times when to the dreamy, studious
Margaret the home circle seemed all discord, all ugly dinginess and
thread-bareness; the struggle for ease and beauty and refinement
seemed hopeless and overwhelming. In these times she would find
herself staring thoughtfully at her mother's face, bent over the mend-
ing basket, or her eyes would leave the chessboard that held her
father's attention so closely, and move from his bald spot, with its
encircling crown of fluffy gray, to his rosy face, with its kind, intent
blue eyes and the little lines about his mouth that his moustache did-
n't hide,—with a half-formed question in her heart. What hadn't they
done, these dearest people, to be always struggling, always tired,
always "behind the game"? Why should they be eternally harassed by
plumbers' bills, and dentists' bills, and shoes that would wear out,
and school-books that must be bought? Why weren't they holding
their place in Weston society, the place to which they were entitled
by right of the Quincy grandfather, and the uncles who were judges?

And in answer Margaret came despondently to the decision, "If you
have children, you never have anything else!" How could Mother
keep up with her friends, when for some fifteen years she had been
far too busy to put on a dainty gown in the afternoon, and serve a
hospitable cup of tea on the east porch? Mother was buttering bread
for supper, then; opening little beds and laying out little nightgowns,
starting Ted off for the milk, washing small hands and faces, soothing bumps and binding cuts, admonishing, praising, directing.
Mother was only too glad to sink wearily into her rocker after dinner, and, after a few spirited visits to the rampant nursery upstairs,
express the hope that nobody would come in to-night. Gradually the
friends dropped away, and the social life of Weston flowed smoothly
on without the Pagets.

But when Margaret began to grow up, she grasped the situation with
all the keenness of a restless and ambitious nature. Weston, detested

Weston, it must apparently be. Very well, she would make the best of Weston. Margaret called on her mother's old friends; she was tireless in charming little attentions. Her own first dances had not been successful; she and Bruce were not good dancers, Margaret had not been satisfied with her gowns, they both felt out of place. When Julie's dancing days came along, Margaret saw to it that everything was made much easier. She planned social evenings at home, and exhausted herself preparing for them, that Julie might know the "right people." To her mother all people were alike, if they were kind and not vulgar; Margaret felt very differently. It was a matter of the greatest satisfaction to her when Julie blossomed into a fluffy-haired butterfly, tremendously in demand, in spite of much-cleaned slippers and often-pressed frocks. Margaret arranged Christmas theatricals, May picnics, Fourth of July gatherings. She never failed Bruce when this dearest brother wanted her company; she was, as Mrs. Paget told her over and over, "the sweetest daughter any woman ever had." But deep in her heart she knew moods of bitter distaste and restlessness. The struggle did not seem worth the making; the odds against her seemed too great.

Still dreaming in the winter dark, she went through the home gate, and up the porch steps of a roomy, cheap house that had been built in the era of scalloped and pointed shingles, of colored glass embellishments around the window-panes, of perforated scroll work and wooden railings in Grecian designs. A mass of wet over-shoes lay on the porch, and two or three of the weather-stained porch rockers swayed under the weight of spread wet raincoats. Two opened umbrellas wheeled in the current of air that came around the house; the porch ran water. While Margaret was adding her own rainy-day equipment to the others, a golden brown setter, one ecstatic wriggle from nose to tail, flashed into view, and came fawning to her feet.

"Hello, Bran!" Margaret said, propping herself against the house with one hand, while she pulled at a tight overshoe. "Hello, old fellow! Well, did they lock him out?"

She let herself and a freezing gust of air into the dark hall, groping to the hat-rack for matches. While she was lighting the gas, a very pretty girl of sixteen, with crimson cheeks and tumbled soft dark hair, came to the dining-room door. This was her sister Julie, Margaret's roommate and warmest admirer, and for the last year or two her inseparable companion. Julie had her finger in a book, but now she closed it, and said affectionately between her yawns: "Come in here, darling! You must be dead."

"Don't let Bran in," cried some one from upstairs.

"He is in, Mother!" Margaret called back, and Rebecca and the three small boys—Theodore, the four-year-old baby, Robert, and Duncan, a grave little lad of seven—all rushed out of the dining-room together, shouting, as they fell on the delighted dog:—

"Aw, leave him in! Aw, leave the poor little feller in! Come on, Bran, come on, old feller! Leave him in, Mark, can't we?"

Kissing and hugging the dog, and stumbling over each other and over him, they went back to the dining-room, which was warm and stuffy. A coal fire was burning low in the grate, the window-panes were beaded, and the little boys had marked their initials in the steam. They had also pushed the fringed table-cover almost off, and scattered the contents of a box of "Lotto" over the scarred walnut top. The room was shabby, ugly, comfortable. Julie and Margaret had established a tea table in the bay window, had embroidered a cover for the wide couch, had burned the big wooden bowl that was supposedly always full of nuts or grapes or red apples. But these touches were lost in the mass of less pleasing detail. The "body Brussels" carpet was worn, the wall paper depressing, the woodwork was painted dark brown, with an imitation burl smeared in by the painter's thumb. The chairs were of several different woods and patterns, the old black walnut sideboard clumsy and battered. About the fire stood some comfortable worn chairs. Margaret dropped wearily into one of these, and the dark-eyed Julie hung over her with little affectionate attentions. The children returned to their game.

"Well, what a time you had with little Dolly Scott!" said Julie, sympathetically. "Ted's been getting it all mixed up! Tell us about it. Poor old Mark, you're all in, aren't you? Mark, would you like a cup of tea?"

"Love it!" Margaret said, a little surprised, for this luxury was not common.

"And toast—we'll toast it!" said Theodore, enthusiastically.

"No, no—no tea!" said Mrs. Paget, coming in at this point with some sewing in her hands. "Don't spoil your dinner, now, Mark dear; tea doesn't do you any good. And I think Blanche is saving the cream for an apple tapioca. Theodore, Mother wants you to go right downstairs for some coal, dear. And, Julie, you'd better start your table; it's close to six. Put up the game, Rebecca!"

There was general protest. Duncan, it seemed, needed only "two more" to win. Little Robert, who was benevolently allowed by the other children to play the game exactly as he pleased, screamed delightedly that he needed only one more, and showed a card upon which even the blank spaces were lavishly covered with glass. He was generously conceded the victory, and kissed by Rebecca and Julie as he made his way to his mother's lap.

"Why, this can't be Robert Paget!" said Mrs. Paget, putting aside her sewing to gather him in her arms. "Not this great, big boy!"

"Yes, I am!" the little fellow asserted joyously, dodging her kisses.

"Good to get home!" Margaret said luxuriously.

"You must sleep late in the morning," her mother commanded affectionately.

"Yes, because you have to be fresh for the party Monday!" exulted Julie. She had flung a white cloth over the long table, and was putting the ringed napkins down with rapid bangs. "And New Year's Eve's the dance!" she went on buoyantly. "I just love Christmas, anyway!"

"Rebecca, ask Blanche if she needs me,"—that was Mother.

"You'd go perfectly crazy about her, Ju, she's the most fascinating, and the most unaffected woman!" Margaret was full of the day's real event.

"And Mother theth that Ted and Dunc and I can have our friendth in on the day after Chrithmath to thee the Chrithmath tree!" That was Rebecca, who added, "Blanche theth no, Mother, unleth you want to make thom cream gravy for the chopth!"

"And, Mark, Eleanor asked if Bruce and you and I weren't going as Pierrot and Pierettes; she's simply crazy to find out!" This was Julie again; and then Margaret, coaxingly, "Do make cream gravy for Bruce, Mother. Give Baby to me!" and little Robert's elated "I know three things Becky's going to get for Christmas, Mark!"

"Well, I think I will, there's milk," Mrs. Paget conceded, rising. "Put Bran out, Teddy; or put him in the laundry if you want to, while we have dinner." Margaret presently followed her mother into the kitchen, stopping in a crowded passageway to tie an apron over her school gown.

"Bruce come in yet?" she said in a low voice.

Her mother flashed her a sympathetic look.

"I don't believe he's coming, Mark."

"Isn't! Oh, Mother! Oh, Mother, does he feel so badly about Betty?"

"I suppose so!" Mrs. Paget went on with her bread cutting.

"But, Mother, surely he didn't expect to marry Betty Forsythe?"

"I don't know why not, Mark. She's a sweet little thing."

"But, Mother—" Margaret was a little at a loss. "We don't seem old enough to really be getting married!" she said, a little lamely.

"Brucie came in about half-past five, and said he was going over to Richie's," Mrs. Paget said, with a sigh.

"In all this rain—that long walk!" Margaret ejaculated, as she filled a long wicker basket with sliced bread.

"I think an evening of work with Richie will do him a world of good," said his mother. There was a pause. "There's Dad. I'll go in," she said, suddenly ending it, as the front door slammed.

Margaret went in, too, to kiss her father; a tired-looking, gray haired man close to fifty, who had taken her chair by the fire. Mrs. Paget was anxious to be assured that his shoulders and shoes were not damp.

"But your hands are icy, Daddy," said she, as she sat down behind a smoking tureen at the head of the table. "Come, have your nice hot soup, dear. Pass that to Dad, Becky, and light the other gas. What sort of a day?"

"A hard day," said Mr. Paget, heavily. "Here, one of you girls put Baby into his chair. Let go, Bob,—I'm too tired to-night for monkey shines!" He sat down stiffly. "Where's Bruce? Can't that boy remember what time we have dinner?"

"Bruce is going to have supper with Richie Williams, Dad," said Mrs. Paget, serenely. "They'll get out their blue prints afterwards and have a good evening's work. Fill the glasses before you sit down, Ju. Come, Ted—put that back on the mantel.—Come, Becky! Tell Daddy about what happened to-day, Mark—"

They all drew up their chairs. Robert, recently graduated from a high chair, was propped upon "The Officers of the Civil War," and "The Household Book of Verse." Julie tied on his bib, and kissed the back of his fat little neck, before she slipped into her own seat. The mother sat between Ted and Duncan, for reasons that immediately became obvious. Margaret sat by her father, and attended to his needs, telling him all about the day, and laying her pretty slim hand over his as it rested beside his plate. The chops and cream gravy, as well as a mountain of baked potatoes, and various vegetables, were under discussion, when every one stopped short in surprise at hearing the doorbell ring.

"Who—?" said Margaret, turning puzzled brows to her mother, and "I'm sure I—" her mother answered, shaking her head. Ted was heard to mutter uneasily that, gee, maybe it was old Pembroke, mad because the fellers had soaked his old skate with snowballs; Julie dimpled and said, "Maybe it's flowers!" Robert shouted, "Bakeryman!" more because he had recently acquired the word than because of any conviction on the subject. In the end Julie went to the door, with the four children in her wake. When she came back, she looked bewildered, and the children a little alarmed.

"It's—it's Mrs. Carr-Boldt, Mother," said Julie.

"Well, don't leave her standing there in the cold, dear!" Mrs. Paget said, rising quickly, to go into the hall. Margaret, her heart thumping with an unanalyzed premonition of something pleasant, and nervous, too, for the hospitality of the Pagets, followed her. So they were all presently crowded into the hall, Mrs. Paget all hospitality, Margaret full of a fear she would have denied that her mother would not be equal to the occasion, the children curious, Julie a little embarrassed.

The visitor, fur-clad, rain-spattered,—for it was raining again,—and beaming, stretched a hand to Mrs. Paget.

"You're Mrs. Paget, of course,—this is an awful hour to interrupt you," she said in her big, easy way, "and there's my Miss Paget,—how do you do? But you see I must get up to town to-night—in this door? I can see perfectly, thank you!—and I did want a little talk with you first. Now, what a shame!"—for the gas, lighted by Theodore at this point, revealed Duncan's bib, and the napkins some of the others were still carrying. "I've interrupted your dinner! Won't you let me wait here until—"

"Perhaps—if you haven't had your supper—you will have some with us," said Mrs. Paget, a little uncertainly. Margaret inwardly shuddered, but Mrs. Carr-Boldt was gracious.

"Mrs. Paget, that's charming of you," she said. "But I had tea at Dayton, and mustn't lose another moment. I shan't dine until I get home. I'm the busiest woman in the world, you know. Now, it won't take me two minutes—"

She was seated now, her hands still deep in her muff, for the parlor was freezing cold. Mrs. Paget, with a rather bewildered look, sat down, too.

"You can run back to your dinners," said she to the children. "Take them, Julie. Mark, dear, will you help the pudding?" They all filed dutifully out of the room, and Margaret, excited and curious, continued a meal that might have been of sawdust and sand for all she knew. The strain did not last long; in about ten minutes Mrs. Paget looked into the room, with a rather worried expression, and said, a little breathlessly:—

"Daddy, can you come here a moment?—You're all right, dear," she added, as Mr. Paget indicated with an embarrassed gesture his well worn house-coat. They went out together. The young people sat almost without speaking, listening to the indistinguishable murmur from the adjoining room, and smiling mysteriously at each other. Then Margaret was called, and went as far as the dining-room door, and came back to put her napkin uncertainly down at her place, hesitated, arranged her gown carefully, and finally went out again. They heard her voice with the others in the parlor... questioning... laughing.

Presently the low murmur broke into audible farewells; chairs were pushed back, feet scraped in the hall.

"Good-night, then!" said Mrs. Carr-Boldt's clear tones, "and so sorry to have—Good-night, Mr. Paget!—Oh, thank you—but I'm well wrapped. Thank you! Good-night, dear! I'll see you again soon—I'll write."

And then came the honking of the motor-car, and a great swish where it grazed a wet bush near the house. Somebody lowered the gas in the hall, and Mrs. Paget's voice said regretfully, "I wish we had had a fire in the parlor—just one of the times!—but there's no help for it." They all came in, Margaret flushed, starry-eyed; her father and mother a little serious. The three blinked at the brighter light, and fell upon the cooling chops as if eating were the important business of the moment.

"We waited the pudding," said Julie. "What is it?"

"Why—" Mrs. Paget began, hesitatingly. Mr. Paget briskly took the matter out of her hands.

"This lady," he said, with an air of making any further talk unnecessary, "needs a secretary, and she has offered your sister Margaret the position. That's the whole affair in a nutshell. I'm not at all sure that your mother and I think it a wise offer for Margaret to accept, and I want to say here and now that I don't want any child of mine to speak of this matter, or make it a matter of general gossip in the neighborhood. Mother, I'd like very much to have Blanche make me a fresh cup of tea."

"Wants Margaret!" gasped Julie, unaffected—so astonishing was the news—by her father's unusual sternness. "Oh, Mother! Oh, Mark! Oh, you lucky thing! When is she coming down here?"

"She isn't coming down here—she wants Mark to go to her—that's it," said her mother.

"Mark—in New York!" shrilled Theodore. Julie got up to rush around the table and kiss her sister; the younger children laughed and shouted.

"There is no occasion for all this," said Mr. Paget, but mildly, for the fresh tea had arrived. "Just quiet them down, will you, Mother? I see nothing very extraordinary in the matter. This Mrs.—Mrs. Carr Boldt—is it?—needs a secretary and companion; and she offers the position to Mark."

"But—but she never even saw Mark until to-day!" marvelled Julie.

"I hardly see how that affects it, my dear!" her father observed unenthusiastically.

"Why, I think it makes it simply extraordinary!" exulted the generous little sister. "Oh, Mark, isn't this just the sort of thing you would
have wished to happen! Secretary work,—just what you love to do!
And you, with your beautiful handwriting, you'll just be invaluable
to her! And your German—and I'll bet you'll just have them all ador-
ing you—!"

"Oh, Ju, if I only can do it!" burst from Margaret, with a little childish gasp. She was sitting back from the table, twisted about so that
she sat sideways, her hands clasped about the top bar of her chair-
back. Her tawny soft hair was loosened about her face, her dark eyes
aflame. "Lenox, she said," Margaret went on dazedly; "and Europe,
and travelling everywhere! And a hundred dollars a month, and nothing to spend it on, so I can still help out here! Why, it—I can't believe
it!"—she looked from one smiling, interested face to another, and
suddenly her radiance underwent a quick eclipse. Her lip trembled,
and she tried to laugh as she pushed her chair back, and ran to the
arms her mother opened. "Oh, Mother!" sobbed Margaret, clinging
there, "do you want me to go—shall I go? I've always been so happy
here, and I feel so ashamed of being discontented,—and I don't
deserve a thing like this to happen to me!"

"Why, God bless her heart!" said Mrs. Paget, tenderly, "of course
you'll go!"

"Oh, you silly! I'll never speak to you again if you don't!" laughed
Julie, through sympathetic tears.

Theodore and Duncan immediately burst into a radiant reminis-
cence of their one brief visit to New York; Rebecca was heard to murmur that she would "vithet Mark thome day"; and the baby, tugging
at his mother's elbow, asked sympathetically if Mark was naughty,
and was caught between his sister's and his mother's arms and kissed

by them both. Mr. Paget, picking his paper from the floor beside his chair, took an arm-chair by the fire, stirred the coals noisily, and while cleaning his glasses, observed rather huskily that the little girl always knew, she could come back again if anything went wrong.

"But suppose I don't suit?" suggested Margaret, sitting back on her heels, refreshed by tears, and with her arms laid across her mother's lap.

"Oh, you'll suit," said Julie, confidently; and Mrs. Paget smoothed the girl's hair back and said affectionately, "I don't think she'll find many girls like you for the asking, Mark!"

"Reading English with the two little girls," said Margaret, dreamily, "and answering notes and invitations. And keeping books—"

"You can do that anyway," said her father, over his paper.

"And dinner lists, you know, Mother—doesn't it sound like an English story!" Margaret stopped in the middle of an ecstatic wriggle. "Mother, will you pray I succeed?" she said solemnly.

"Just be your own dear simple self, Mark," her mother advised. "January!" she added, with a great sigh. "It's the first break, isn't it, Dad? Think of trying to get along without our Mark!"

"January!" Julie was instantly alert. "Why, but you'll need all sorts of clothes!"

"Oh, she says there's a sewing woman always in the house," Margaret said, almost embarrassed by the still-unfolding advantages of the proposition. "I can have her do whatever's left over." Her father lowered his paper to give her a shrewd glance.

"I suppose somebody knows something about this Mrs. Carr-Boldt, Mother?" asked he. "She's all right, I suppose?"

"Oh, Dad, her name's always in the papers," Julie burst out; and the mother smiled as she said, "We'll be pretty sure of everything before we let our Mark go!" Later, when the children had been dismissed, and he himself was going, rather stiffly, toward the stairs, Mr. Paget again voiced a mild doubt.

"There was a perfectly good reason for her hurry, I suppose? Old secretary deserted—got married—? She had good reason for wanting Mark in all this hurry?"

Mrs. Paget and her daughters had settled about the fire for an hour's delicious discussion, but she interrupted it to say soothingly, "It was her cousin, Dad, who's going to be married, and she's been trying to get hold of just the right person—she says she's fearfully behind-hand—"

"Well, you know best," said Mr. Paget, departing a little discontentedly.

Left to the dying fire, the others talked, yawned, made a pretence of breaking up: talked and yawned again. The room grew chilly. Bruce,- oldest of the children,—dark, undemonstrative, weary,—presently came in, and was given the news, and marvelled in his turn. Bruce and Margaret had talked of their ambitions a hundred times: of the day when he might enter college and when she might find the leisure and beauty in life for which her soul hungered. Now, as he sat with his arm about her, and her head on his shoulder, he said with generous satisfaction over and over:—

"It was coming to you, Mark; you've earned it!"

At midnight, loitering upstairs, cold and yawning, Margaret kissed her mother and brother quietly, with whispered brief good-nights. But Julie, lying warm and snug in bed half-an-hour later, had a last word.

"You know, Mark, I think I'm as happy as you are—no, I'm not generous at all! It's just that it makes me feel that things do come your way finally, if you wait long enough, and that we aren't the only family in town that never has anything decent happen to it!... I'll miss you awfully, Mark, darling!... Mark, do you suppose Mother'd let me take this bed out, and just have a big couch in here? It would make the room seem so much bigger. And then I could have the girls come up here, don't you know—when they came over.... Think of you— you—going abroad! I'd simply die! I can't wait to tell Betty!... I hope to goodness Mother won't put Beck in here!... We've had this room a long time together, haven't we? Ever since Grandma died. Do you remember her canary, that Teddy hit with a plate?... I'm going to miss you terribly, Mark. But we'll write...."

CHAPTER III

On the days that followed, the miracle came to be accepted by all Weston, which was much excited for a day or two over this honor done a favorite daughter, and by all the Pagets,—except Margaret. Margaret went through the hours in her old, quiet manner, a little more tender and gentle perhaps than she had been; but her heart never beat normally, and she lay awake late at night, and early in the morning, thinking, thinking, thinking. She tried to realize that it was in her honor that a farewell tea was planned at the club, it was for her that her fellow-teachers were planning a good-bye luncheon; it was really she—Margaret Paget—whose voice said at the telephone a dozen times a day, "On the fourteenth.—Oh, do I? I don't feel calm! Can't you try to come in—I do want to see you before I go!" She dutifully repeated Bruce's careful directions; she was to give her check to an expressman, and her suitcase to a red-cap; the expressman would probably charge fifty cents, the red-cap was to have no more than fifteen. And she was to tell the latter to put her into a taxicab.

"I'll remember," Margaret assured him gratefully, but with a sense of unreality pressing almost painfully upon her.—One of a million ordinary school teachers, in a million little towns—and this marvel had befallen her!

The night of the Pagets' Christmas play came, a night full of laughter and triumph; and marked for Margaret by the little parting gifts that were slipped into her hands, and by the warm good wishes that were murmured, not always steadily, by this old friend and that. When the time came to distribute plates and paper napkins, and great saucers of ice cream and sliced cake, Margaret was toasted in cold sweet lemonade; and drawing close together to "harmonize" more perfectly, the circle about her touched their glasses while they sang, "For she's a jolly good fellow." Later, when the little supper was almost over, Ethel Elliot, leaning over to lay her hand on Margaret's, began in her rich contralto:—

" When other lips and other hearts..."

and as they all went seriously through the two verses, they stood up, one by one, and linked arms; the little circle, affectionate and admiring, that had bounded Margaret's friendships until now.

Then Christmas came, with a dark, freezing walk to the pine-spiced and candle-lighted early service in the little church, and a quicker walk home, chilled and happy and hungry, to a riotous Christmas breakfast, and a littered breakfast table. The new year came, with a dance and revel, and the Pagets took one of their long tramps through the snowy afternoon, and came back hungry for a big dinner. Then there was dressmaking,—Mrs. Schmidt in command, Mrs. Paget tireless at the machine, Julie all eager interest. Margaret, patiently standing to be fitted, conscious of the icy, wet touch of Mrs. Schmidt's red fingers on her bare arms, dreamily acquiescent as to buttons or hooks, was totally absent in spirit.

A trunk came, Mr. Paget very anxious that the keys should not be "fooled with" by the children. Margaret's mother packed this trunk scientifically. "No, now the shoes, Mark—now that heavy skirt," she would say. "Run get mother some more tissue paper, Beck. You'll have to leave the big cape, dear, and you can send for it if you need it. Now the blue dress, Ju. I think that dyed so prettily, just the thing for mornings. And here's your prayer book in the tray, dear; if you go Saturday you'll want it the first thing in the morning. See, I'll put a fresh handkerchief in it—"

Margaret, relaxed and idle, in a rocker, with Duncan in her lap busily working at her locket, would say over and over:—

"You're all such angels,—I'll never forget it!" and wish that, knowing how sincerely she meant it, she could feel it a little more. Conversation languished in these days; mother and daughters feeling that time was too precious to waste speech of little things, and that their hearts were too full to touch upon the great change impending.

A night came when the Pagets went early upstairs, saying that, after all, it was not like people marrying and going to Russia; it was not like a real parting; it wasn't as if Mark couldn't come home again in four hours if anything went wrong at either end of the line. Margaret's heart was beating high and quick now; she tried to show some of the love and sorrow she knew she should have felt, she knew that she did feel under the hurry of her blood that made speech impossible. She went to her mother's door, slender and girlish in her white nightgown, to kiss her good-night again. Mrs. Paget's big arms went about her daughter. Margaret laid her head childishly on her mother's shoulder. Nothing of significance was said. Margaret whispered, "Mother, I love you!" Her mother said, "You were such a little thing, Mark, when I kissed you one day, without hugging you, and you said, 'Please don't love me just with your face, Mother, love me with your heart!'" Then she added, "Did you and Julie get that extra blanket down to-day, dear?—it's going to be very cold." Margaret nodded. "Good-night, little girl—" "Goodnight, Mother—"

That was the real farewell, for the next morning was all confusion. They dressed hurriedly, by chilly gas-light; clocks were compared, Rebecca's back buttoned; Duncan's overcoat jerked on; coffee drunk scalding hot as they stood about the kitchen table; bread barely tasted. They walked to the railway station on wet sidewalks, under a broken sky, Bruce, with Margaret's suit-case, in the lead. Weston was asleep in the gray morning, after the storm. Far and near belated cocks were crowing.

A score of old friends met Margaret at the train; there were gifts, promises, good wishes. There came a moment when it was generally felt that the Pagets should be left alone, now—the far whistle of the train beyond the bridge—the beginning of good-byes—a sudden filling of the mother's eyes that was belied by her smile.—"Good-bye, sweetest—don't knock my hat off, baby dear! Beck, darling—Oh, Ju, do! don't just say it—start me a letter to-night! ALL write to me! Good-bye, Dad, darling,—all right, Bruce, I'll get right in!—another for Dad. Good-bye, Mother darling,—goodbye! Good-bye!"

Then for the Pagets there was a walk back to the empty disorder of the house: Julie very talkative, at her father's side; Bruce walking far behind the others with his mother,—and the day's familiar routine to be somehow gone through without Margaret.

But for Margaret, settling herself comfortably in the grateful warmth of the train, and watching the uncertain early sunshine brighten unfamiliar fields and farmhouses, every brilliant possibility in life seemed to be waiting. She tried to read, to think, to pray, to stare steadily out of the window; she could do nothing for more than a moment at a time. Her thoughts went backward and forward like a weaving shuttle: "How good they've all been to me! How grateful I am! Now if only, only, I can make good!"

"Look out for the servants!" Julie, from the depth of her sixteen years-old wisdom had warned her sister. "The governess will hate you because she'll be afraid you'll cut her out, and Mrs. Carr-Boldt's maid will be a cat! They always are, in books."

Margaret had laughed at this advice, but in her heart she rather believed it. Her new work seemed so enchanting to her that it was not easy to believe that she did not stand in somebody's light. She was glad that by a last-moment arrangement she was to arrive at the Grand Central Station at almost the same moment as Mrs. Carr-Boldt herself, who was coming home from a three-weeks' visit in the middle west. Margaret gave only half her attention to the flying country that was beginning to shape itself into streets and rows of houses; all the last half hour of the trip was clouded by the nervous fear that she would somehow fail to find Mrs. Carr-Boldt in the confusion at the railroad terminal.

But happily enough the lady was found without trouble, or rather Margaret was found, felt an authoritative tap on her shoulder, caught a breath of fresh violets, and a glimpse of her patron's clear skinned, resolute face. They whirled through wet deserted streets; Mrs. Carr-Boldt gracious and talkative, Margaret nervously interested and amused.

Their wheels presently grated against a curb, a man in livery opened the limousine door. Margaret saw an immense stone mansion facing the park, climbed a dazzling flight of wide steps, and was in a great hall that faced an interior court, where there were Florentine marble benches, and the great lifted leaves of palms. She was a little dazed by crowded impressions; impressions of height and spaciousness and richness, and opening vistas; a great marble stairway, and a landing where there was an immense designed window in clear leaded glass; rugs, tapestries, mirrors, polished wood and great chairs with brocaded seats and carved dark backs. Two little girls, heavy, well groomed little girls,—one spectacled and good-natured looking, the other rather pretty, with a mass of fair hair,—were coming down the stairs with an eager little German woman. They kissed their mother, much diverted by the mad rushes and leaps of the two white poodles who accompanied them.

"These are my babies, Miss Paget," said Mrs. Carr-Boldt. "This is Victoria, who's eleven, and Harriet, who's six. And these are Monsieur—"

"Monsieur Patou and Monsieur Mouche," said Victoria, introducing the dogs with entire ease of manner. The German woman said something forcibly, and Margaret understood the child's reply in that tongue: "Mamma won't blame you, Fraulein; Harriet and I wished them to come down!"

Presently they all went up in a luxuriously fitted little lift, Margaret being carried to the fourth floor to her own rooms, to which a little maid escorted her.

When the maid had gone Margaret walked to the door and tried it, for no reason whatever; it was shut. Her heart was beating violently. She walked into the middle of the room and looked at herself in the mirror, and laughed a little breathless laugh. Then she took off her hat carefully and went into the bedroom that was beyond her sitting room, and hung her hat in a fragrant white closet that was entirely and delightfully empty, and put her coat on a hanger, and her gloves and bag in the empty big top drawer of a great mahogany bureau. Then she went back to the mirror and looked hard at her own beauty reflected in it; and laughed her little laugh again.

"It's too good—it's too much!" she whispered.

She investigated her domain, after quelling a wild desire to sit down at the beautiful desk and try the new pens, the crystal ink-well, and the heavy paper, with its severely engraved address, in a long letter to Mother.

There was a tiny upright piano in the sitting-room, and at the fire-place a deep thick rug, and an immense leather arm-chair. A clock in crystal and gold flanked by two crystal candlesticks had the centre of the mantelpiece. On the little round mahogany centre table was a lamp with a wonderful mosaic shade; a little book-case was filled with books and magazines. Margaret went to one of the three win-dows, and looked down upon the bare trees and the snow in the park, and upon the rumbling green omnibuses, all bathed in bright chilly sunlight.

A mahogany door with a crystal knob opened into the bedroom, where there was a polished floor, and more rugs, and a gay rosy wall paper, and a great bed with a lace cover. Beyond was a bathroom, all enamel, marble, glass, and nickel-plate, with heavy monogrammed towels on the rack, three new little wash-cloths sealed in glazed paper, three new tooth-brushes in paper cases, and a cake of famous English soap just out of its wrapper.

Over the whole little suite there brooded an exquisite order. Not a particle of dust broke the shining surfaces of the mahogany, not a fallen leaf lay under the great bowl of roses on the desk. Now and then the radiator clanked in the stress; it was hard to believe in that warmth and silence that a cold winter wind was blowing outside, and that snow still lay on the ground.

Margaret, resting luxuriously in the big chair, became thoughtful; presently she went into the bedroom, and knelt down beside the bed.

"O Lord, let me stay here," she prayed, her face in her hands. "I want so to stay—make me a success!"

Never was a prayer more generously answered. Miss Paget was an instant success. In something less than two months she became indis-pensable to Mrs. Carr-Boldt, and was a favorite with every one, from the rather stolid, silent head of the house down to the least of the maids. She was so busy, so unaffected, so sympathetic, that her sudden rise in favor was resented by no one. The butler told her his troubles, the French maid darkly declared that but for Miss Paget she would not for one second r-r-remain! The children went cheerfully even to the dentist with their adored Miss Peggy; they soon preferred her escort to matinee or zoo to that of any other person. Margaret also escorted Mrs. Carr-Boldt's mother, a magnificent old lady, on shopping expeditions, and attended the meetings of charity boards for Mrs. Carr-Boldt. With notes and invitations, account books and cheque books, dinner lists, and interviews with caterers, decorators, and florists, Margaret's time was full, but she loved every moment of her work, and gloried in her increasing usefulness.

At first there were some dark days; notably the dreadful one upon which Margaret somehow—somewhere—dropped the box containing the new hat she was bringing home for Harriet, and kept the little girl out in the cold afternoon air while the motor made a fruitless trip back to the milliner's. Harriet contracted a cold, and Harriet's mother for the first time spoke severely to Margaret. There was another bad day when Margaret artlessly admitted to Mrs. Pierre Polk at the telephone that Mrs. Carr-Boldt was not engaged for dinner that evening, thus obliging her employer to snub the lady, or accept a distasteful invitation to dine. And there was a most uncomfortable occasion when Mr. Carr-Boldt, not at all at his best, stumbled in upon his wife with some angry observations meant for her ear alone; and Margaret, busy with accounts in a window recess, was, unknown to them both, a distressed witness.

"Another time, Miss Paget," said Mrs. Carr-Boldt, coldly, upon Margaret's appearing scarlet-cheeked between the curtains, "don't oblige me to ascertain that you are not within hearing before feeling sure of privacy. Will you finish those bills upstairs, if you please?"

Margaret went upstairs with a burning heart, cast her bills haphazard on her own desk, and flung herself, dry-eyed and furious, on the bed. She was far too angry to think, but lay there for perhaps twenty minutes with her brain whirling. Finally rising, she brushed up her hair, straightened her collar, and, full of tremendous resolves, stepped into her little sitting room, to find Mrs. Carr-Boldt in the big chair, serenely eyeing her.

"I'm so sorry I spoke so, Peggy," said her employer, generously. "But the truth is, I am not myself when—when Mr. Carr-Boldt—" The little hesitating appeal in her voice completely disarmed Margaret. In the end the little episode cemented the rapidly growing friendship between the two women, Mrs. Carr-Boldt seeming to enjoy the relief of speaking rather freely of what was the one real trial in her life.

"My husband has always had too much money," she said, in her positive way. "At one time we were afraid that he would absolutely ruin his health by this—habit of his. His physician and I took him around the world,—I left Victoria, just a baby, with mother,—and for too years he was never out of my sight. It has never been so bad since. You know yourself how reliable he usually is," she finished cheerfully, "unless some of the other men get hold of him!"

As the months went on Margaret came to admire her employer more and more. There was not an indolent impulse in Mrs. Carr-Boldt's entire composition. Smooth-haired, fresh-skinned, in spotless linen, she began the day at eight o'clock, full of energy and interest. She had daily sessions with butler and house-keeper, shopped with Margaret and the children, walked about her greenhouse or her country garden with her skirts pinned up, and had tulips potted and stone work continued. She was prominent in several clubs, a famous dinner-giver, she took a personal interest in all her servants, loved to settle their quarrels and have three or four of them up on the carpet at once, tearful and explanatory. Margaret kept for her a list of some two hundred friends, whose birthdays were to be marked with carefully selected gifts. She pleased Mrs. Carr-Boldt by her open amazement at the latter's vitality. The girl observed that her employer could not visit any institution without making a few vigorous suggestions as she went about, she accompanied her cheques to the organized chari-ties—and her charity flowed only through absolutely reliable chan-nels—with little friendly, advisory letters. She liked the democratic attitude for herself,—even while promptly snubbing any such ten-dency in children or friends;—and told Margaret that she only used her coat of arms on house linen, stationery, and livery, because her husband and mother liked it. "It's of course rather nice to realize that one comes from one of the oldest of the Colonial families," she would say. "The Carterets of Maryland, you know.—But it's all such bosh!"

And she urged Margaret to claim her own right to family honors: "You're a Quincy, my dear! Don't let that woman intimidate you,— she didn't remember that her grandfather was a captain until her hus-band made his money. And where the family portraits came from I don't know, but I think there's a man on Fourth Avenue who does 'em!" she would say, or, "I know all about Lilly Reynolds, Peggy. Her father was as rich as she says, and I daresay the crest is theirs. But ask her what her maternal grandmother did for a living, if you want to shut her up!" Other people she would condemn with a mere whis-pered "Coal!" or "Patent bath-tubs!" behind her fan, and it pleased her to tell people that her treasure of a secretary had the finest blood in the world in her veins. Margaret was much admired, and Margaret was her discovery, and she liked to emphasize her find.

Mrs. Carr-Boldt's mother, a tremulous, pompous old lady, unwit-tingly aided the impression by taking an immense fancy to Margaret, and by telling her few intimates and the older women among her daughter's friends that the girl was a perfect little thoroughbred. When the Carr-Boldts filled their house with the reckless and noisy company they occasionally affected, Mrs. Carteret would say majestically to Margaret:—

"You and I have nothing in common with this riff-raff, my dear!"

Summer came, and Margaret headed a happy letter "Bar Harbor." Two months later all Weston knew that Margaret Paget was going abroad for a year with those rich people, and had written her mother from the Lusitania. Letters from London, from Germany, from Holland, from Russia, followed. "We are going to put the girls at school in Switzerland, and (ahem!) winter on the Riviera, and then Rome for Holy Week!" she wrote.

She was presently home again, chattering French and German to amuse her father, teaching Becky a little Italian song to match her little Italian costume.

"It's wonderful to me how you get along with all these rich people, Mark," said her mother, admiringly, during Margaret's home visit. Mrs. Paget was watering the dejected-looking side garden with a straggling length of hose; Margaret and Julie shelling peas on the side steps. Margaret laughed, coloring a little.

"Why, we're just as good as they are, Mother!"

Mrs. Paget drenched a dried little dump of carnations.

"We're as good," she admitted; "but we're not as rich, or as travelled,—we haven't the same ideas; we belong to a different class."

"Oh, no, we don't, Mother," Margaret said quickly. "Who are the Carr Boldts, except for their money? Why, Mrs. Carteret,—for all her family!—isn't half the aristocrat Grandma was! And you—you could be a Daughter of The Officers of the Revolution, Mother!"

"Why, Mark, I never heard that!" her mother protested, cleaning the sprinkler with a hairpin.

"Mother!" Julie said eagerly. "Great-grandfather Quincy!"

"Oh, Grandpa," said Mrs. Paget. "Yes, Grandpa was a paymaster. He was on Governor Hancock's staff. They used to call him 'Major.' But Mark- " she turned off the water, holding her skirts away from the combination of mud and dust underfoot, "that's a very silly way to talk, dear! Money does make a difference; it does no good to go back into the past and say that this one was a judge and that one a major; we must live our lives where we are!"

Margaret had not lost a wholesome respect for her mother's opinion in the two years she had been away, but she had lived in a very different world, and was full of new ideas.

"Mother, do you mean to tell me that if you and Dad hadn't had a perfect pack of children, and moved so much, and if Dad—say—had been in that oil deal that he said he wished he had the money for, and we still lived in the brick house, that you wouldn't be in every way the equal of Mrs. Carr-Boldt?"

"If you mean as far as money goes, Mark,—no. We might have been well to-do as country people go, I suppose—"

"Exactly!" said Margaret; "and you would have been as well off as dozens of the people who are going about in society this minute! It's the merest chance that we aren't rich. Just for instance: father's father had twelve children, didn't he?—and left them—how much was it?—about three thousand dollars apiece—"

"And a Godsend it was, too," said her mother, reflectively.

"But suppose Dad had been the only child, Mother," Margaret persisted, "he would have had—"

"He would have had the whole thirty-six thousand dollars, I suppose, Mark."

"Or more," said Margaret, "for Grandfather Paget was presumably spending money on them all the time."

"Well, but, Mark—" said Mrs. Paget, laughing as at the vagaries of a small child, "Father Paget did have twelve children—and Daddy and I eight—" she sighed, as always, at the thought of the little son who was gone,—"and there you are! You can't get away from that, dear."

Margaret did not answer. But she thought to herself that very few people held Mother's views of this subject.

Mrs. Carr-Boldt's friends, for example, did not accept increasing cares in this resigned fashion; their lives were ideally pleasant and harmonious without the complicated responsibilities of large families. They drifted from season to season without care, always free, always gay, always irreproachably gowned. In winter there were daily meetings, for shopping, for luncheon, bridge or tea; summer was filled with a score of country visits. There were motor-trips for week-ends, dinners, theatre, and the opera to fill the evenings, German or singing lessons, manicure, masseuse, and dressmaker to crowd the morning hours all the year round. Margaret learned from these exquisite, fragrant creatures the art of being perpetually fresh and charming, learned their methods of caring for their own beauty, learned to love rare toilet waters and powders, fine embroidered linen and silk stockings. There was no particular strain upon her wardrobe now, nor upon her purse; she could be as dainty as she liked. She listened to the conversations that went on about her,—sometimes critical or unconvinced; more often admiring; and as she listened she found slowly but certainly her own viewpoint. She was not mercenary. She would not marry a man just for his money, she decided, but just as certainly she would not marry a man who could not give her a comfortable establishment, a position in society. The man seemed in no hurry to appear; as a matter of fact, the men whom Margaret met were openly anxious to evade marriage, even with the wealthy girls of their own set. Margaret was not concerned; she was too happy to miss the love-making element; the men she saw were not of a type to inspire a sensible busy, happy, girl with any very deep feeling. And it was with generous and perfect satisfaction that she presently had news of Julie's happy engagement. Julie was to marry a young and popular doctor, the only child of one of Weston's most prominent families. The little sister's letter bubbled joyously with news.

"Harry's father is going to build us a little house on the big place, the darling," wrote Julie; "and we will stay with them until it is done. But in five years Harry says we will have a real honeymoon, in Europe! Think of going to Europe as a married woman! Mark, I wish you could see my ring; it is a beauty, but don't tell Mother I was silly enough to write about it!"

Margaret delightedly selected a little collection of things for Julie's trousseau. A pair of silk stockings, a scarf she never had worn, a lace petticoat, pink silk for a waist. Mrs. Carr-Boldt, coming in in the midst of these preparations, insisted upon adding so many other things, from trunks and closets, that Margaret was speechless with delight. Scarves, cobwebby silks in uncut lengths, embroidered lingerie still in the tissue paper of Paris shops, parasols, gloves, and lengths of lace,—she piled all of them into Margaret's arms. Julie's trousseau was consequently quite the most beautiful Weston had ever seen; and the little sister's cloudless joy made the fortnight Margaret spent at home at the time of the wedding a very happy one. It was a time of rush and flurry, laughter and tears, of roses, and girls in white gowns. But some ten days before the wedding, Julie and Margaret happened to be alone for a peaceful hour over their sewing, and fell to talking seriously.

"You see, our house will be small," said Julie; "but I don't care—we don't intend to stay in Weston all our lives. Don't breathe this to any one, Mark, but if Harry does as well as he's doing now for two years, we'll rent the little house, and we're going to Baltimore for a year for a special course. Then—you know he's devoted to Dr. McKim, he always calls him 'the chief,'—then he thinks maybe McKim will work him into his practice,—he's getting old, you know, and that means New York!"

"Oh, Ju,—really!"

"I don't see why not," Julie said, dimpling. "Harry's crazy to do it. He says he doesn't propose to live and die in Weston. McKim could throw any amount of hospital practice his way, to begin with. And you know Harry'll have something,—and the house will rent. I'm crazy," said Julie, enthusiastically, "to take one of those lovely old apartments on Washington Square, and meet a few nice people, you know, and really make something of my life!"

"Mrs. Carr-Boldt and I will spin down for you every few days," Margaret said, falling readily in with the plan. "I'm glad you're not going to simply get into a rut the way some of the other girls have,- cooking and babies and nothing else!" she said.

"I think that's an awful mistake," Julie said placidly. "Starting in right is so important. I don't want to be a mere drudge like Ethel or Louise—they may like it. I don't! Of course, this isn't a matter to talk of," she went on, coloring a little. "I'd never breathe this to Mother! But it's perfectly absurd to pretend that girls don't discuss these things. I've talked to Betty and Louise—we all talk about it, you know. And Louise says they haven't had one free second since Buddy came. She can't keep one maid, and she says the idea of two maids eating their three meals a day, whether she's home or not, makes her perfectly sick! Some one's got to be with him every single second, even now, when he's four,—to see that he doesn't fall off something, or put things in his mouth. And as Louise says—it means no more week end trips; you can't go visiting over night, you can't even go for a day's drive or a day on the beach, without extra clothes for the baby, a mosquito-net and an umbrella for the baby—milk packed in ice for the baby—somebody trying to get the baby to take his nap—it's awful! It would end our Baltimore plan, and that means New York, and New York means everything to Harry and me!" finished Julie, contentedly, flattening a finished bit of embroidery on her knee, and regarding it complacently.

"Well, I think you're right," Margaret approved. "Things are different now from what they were in Mother's day."

"And look at Mother," Julie said. "One long slavery! Life's too short to wear yourself out that way!"

Mrs. Paget's sunny cheerfulness was sadly shaken when the actual moment of parting with the exquisite, rose-hatted, gray-frocked Julie came; her face worked pitifully in its effort to smile; her tall figure, awkward in an ill-made unbecoming new silk, seemed to droop tenderly over the little clinging wife. Margaret, stirred by the sight of tears on her mother's face, stood with an arm about her, when the bride and groom drove away in the afternoon sunshine.

"I'm going to stay with you until she gets back!" she reminded her mother. "And you know you've always said you wanted the girls to marry, Mother," urged Mr. Paget. Rebecca felt this a felicitous moment to ask if she and the boys could have the rest of the ice-cream.

"Divide it evenly," said Mrs. Paget, wiping her eyes and smiling. "Yes, I know, Daddy dear, I'm an ungrateful woman! I suppose your turn will come next, Mark, and then I don't know what I will do!"

CHAPTER IV

But Margaret's turn did not come for nearly a year. Then—in Germany again, and lingering at a great Berlin hotel because the spring was so beautiful, and the city so sweet with linden bloom, and especially because there were two Americans at the hotel whose game of bridge it pleased Mr. and Mrs. Carr-Boldt daily to hope they could match,—then Margaret was transformed within a few hours from a merely pretty, very dignified, perfectly contented secretary, entirely satisfied with what she wore as long as it was suitable and fresh, into a living woman, whose cheeks paled and flushed at nothing but her thoughts, who laughed at herself in her mirror, loitered over her toilet trying one gown after another, and walked half-smiling through a succession of rosy dreams.

It all came about very simply. One of the aforementioned bridge players wondered if Mrs. Carr-Bolt and her niece—oh, wasn't it?—her secretary then,—would like to hear a very interesting young American professor lecture this morning?—wondered, when they were fanning themselves in the airy lecture-room, if they would care to meet Professor Tension?

Margaret looked into a pair of keen, humorous eyes, answered with her own smile Professor Tension's sudden charming one, lost her small hand in his big firm one. Then she listened to him talk, as he strode about the platform, boyishly shaking back the hair that fell across his forehead. After that he walked to the hotel with them, through dazzling seas of perfume, and of flowers, under the enchanted shifting green of great trees,—or so Margaret thought. There was a plunge from the hot street into the awning cool gloom of the hotel, and then a luncheon, when the happy steady murmur from their own table seemed echoed by the murmurs clink and stir and laughter all about them, and accented by the not-too-close music from the band.

Doctor Tension was everything charming, Margaret thought, instantly drawn by the unaffected, friendly manner, and watching the interested gleam of his blue eyes and the white flash of his teeth He was a gentleman, to begin with; distinguished at thirty-two in his chosen work; big and well-built, without suggesting the athlete, of an old and honored American family, and the only son of a rich—and eccentric—old doctor whom Mrs. Carr-Bolt chanced to know.

He was frankly delighted at the chance that had brought him in contact with these charming people; and as Mrs. Carr-Bolt took an instant fancy to him, and as he was staying at their own hotel, they saw him after that every day, and several times a day. Margaret would come down the great sun-bathed stairway in the morning to find him patiently waiting in a porch chair. Her heart would give a great leap -half joy, half new strange pain, as she recognized him. There would be time for a chat over their fruit and eggs before Mr. Carr-Bolt came down, all ready for a motor-trip, or Mrs. Carr-Bolt, swathed in cream-colored coat and flying veils, joined them with an approving "Good-morning."

Margaret would remember these breakfasts all her life; the sun splashed little table in a corner of the great dining-room, the rosy fatherly waiter who was so much delighted with her German, the busy picturesque traffic in the street just below the wide-open window. She would always remember a certain filmy silk striped gown, a wide hat loaded with daisies; always love the odor of linden trees in the spring.

Sometimes the professor went with them on their morning drive, to be dropped at the lecture-hall with Margaret and Mrs. Carr-Bolt. The latter was pleased to take the course of lectures very seriously, and carried a handsome Russian leather note-book, and a gold pencil. Sometimes after luncheon they all went on an expedition together, and now and then Margaret and Doctor Tension went off alone on foot, to explore the city. They would end the afternoon with coffee and little cakes in some tea-room, and come home tired and merry in the long shadows of the spring sunset, with wilted flowers from the street markets in their hands.

There was one glorious tramp in the rain, when the professor's great laugh rang out like a boy's for sheer high spirits, and when Margaret was an enchanting vision in her long coat, with her cheeks glowing through the blown wet tendrils of her hair. That day they had tea in the deserted charming little parlor of a tiny inn, and drank it toasting their feet over a glowing fire.

"Is Mrs. Carr-Bolt your mother's or your father's sister?" John Tension asked, watching his companion with approval.

"Oh, good gracious!" said Margaret, laughing over her teacup. "Haven't I told you yet that I'm only her secretary? I never saw Mrs. Carr Bolt until five years ago."

"Perhaps you did tell me. But I got it into my head, that first day, that you were aunt and niece—"

"People do, I think," Margaret said thoughtfully, "because we're both fair." She did not say that but for Mrs. Carr-Bolt's invaluable maid the likeness would have been less marked, on this score at least. "I taught school," she went on simply, "and Mrs. Carr-Bolt happened to come to my school, and she asked me to come to her."

"You're all alone in the world, Miss Page?" He was eyeing her amusingly; the direct question came quite naturally.

"Oh, dear me, no! My father and mother are living"; and feeling, as she always did, a little claim on her loyalty, she added: "We are, or were, rather, Southern people,—but my father settled in a very small New York town—"

"Mrs. Carr-Bolt told me that—I'd forgotten—" said Professor Tenison, and he carried the matter entirely out of Margaret's hands,—much, much further indeed than she would have carried it, by continuing, "She tells me that Quincyport was named for your mother's grandfather, and that Judge Paget was your father's father."

"Father's uncle," Margaret corrected, although as a matter of fact Judge Paget had been no nearer than her father's second cousin. "But father always called him uncle," Margaret assured herself inwardly. To the Quincy-port claim she said nothing. Quincyport was in the county that Mother's people had come from; Quincy was a very unusual name, and the original Quincy had been a Charles, which certainly was one of Mother's family names. Margaret and Julie, browsing about among the colonial histories and genealogies of the Weston Public Library years before, had come to a jubilant certainty that mother's grandfather must have been the same man. But she did not feel quite so positive now.

"Your people aren't still in the South, you said?"

"Oh, no!" Margaret cleared her throat. "They're in Weston—Weston, New York."

"Weston! Not near Dayton?"

"Why, yes! Do you know Dayton?"

"Do I know Dayton?" He was like an eager child. "Why, my Aunt Pamela lives there; the only mother I ever knew! I knew Weston, too, a little. Lovely homes there, some of them,—old colonial houses. And your mother lives there? Is she fond of flowers?"

"She loves them," Margaret said, vaguely uncomfortable.

"Well, she must know Aunt Pamela," said John Tenison, enthusiastically. "I expect they'd be great friends. And you must know Aunt Pam. She's like a dainty old piece of china, or a—I don't know, a tea rose! She's never married, and she lives in the most charming brick house, with brick walls and hollyhocks all about it, and such an atmosphere inside! She has an old maid and an old gardener, and—don't you know—she's the sort of woman who likes to sit down under a portrait of your great-grandfather, in a dim parlor full of mahogany and rose jars, with her black silk skirts spreading about her, and an Old Blue cup in her hand, and talk family,—how cousin this married a man whose people aren't anybody, and cousin that is outraging precedent by naming her child for her husband's side of the house. She's a funny, dear old lady! You know, Miss Paget," the professor went on, with his eager, impersonal air, "when I met you, I thought you didn't quite seem like a New Yorker and a Bar Harborer—if that's the word! Aunt Pam—you know she's my only mother, I got all my early knowledge from her!—Aunt Pam detests the usual New York girl, and the minute I met you I knew she'd like you. You'd sort of fit into the Dayton picture, with your braids, and those ruffly things you wear!"

Margaret said simply, "I would love to meet her," and began slowly to draw on her gloves. It surely was not requisite that she should add, "But you must not confuse my home with any such exquisitely ordered existence as that. We are poor people, our house is crowded, our days a severe and endless struggle with the ugly things of life. We have good blood in our veins, but not more than hundreds of thousands of other American families. My mother would not understand one tenth of your aunt's conversation; your aunt would find very uninteresting the things that are vital to my mother."

No, she couldn't say that. She picked up her dashing little hat, and pinned it over her loosened soft mass of yellow hair, and buttoned up her storm coat, and plunged her hands deep in her pockets. No, the professor would call on her at Bar Harbor, take a yachting trip with the Carr-Boldts perhaps, and then—and then, when they were really good friends, some day she would ask. Mother to have a simple little luncheon, and Mrs. Carr-Boldt would let her bring Dr. Tenison down in the motor from New York. And meantime—no need to be too explicit.

For just two happy weeks Margaret lived in Wonderland. The fourteen days were a revelation to her. Life seemed to grow warmer, more rosy colored. Little things became significant; every moment carried its freight of joy. Her beauty, always notable, became almost startling; there was a new glow in her cheeks and lips, new fire in the dark lashed eyes that were so charming a contrast to her bright hair. Like a pair of joyous and irresponsible children she and John Tenison walked through the days, too happy ever to pause and ask themselves whither they were going.

Then abruptly it ended. Victoria, brought down from school in Switzerland with various indications of something wrong, was in a flash a sick child; a child who must be hurried home to the only surgeon in whom Mrs. Carr-Boldt placed the least trust. There was hurried packing, telephoning, wiring; it was only a few hours after the great German physician's diagnosis that they were all at the railway station, breathless, nervous, eager to get started.

Doctor Tenison accompanied them to the station, and in the five minutes' wait before their train left, a little incident occurred, the memory of which clouded Margaret's dreams for many a day to come. Arriving, as they were departing, were the St. George Allens, noisy, rich, arrogant New Yorkers, for whom Margaret had a special dislike. The Allens fell joyously upon the Carr-Boldt party, with a confusion of greetings. "And Jack Tenison!" shouted Lily Allen, delightedly. "Well, what fun! What are you doing here?"

"I'm feeling a little lonely," said the professor, smiling at Mrs. Carr-Boldt.

"Nothing like that; unsay them woyds," said Maude Allen, cheerfully. "Mamma, make him dine with us! Say you will."

"I assure you I was dreading the lonely evening," John Tenison said gratefully. Margaret's last glimpse of his face was between Lily's pink and cherry hat, and Maude's astonishing headgear of yellow straw, gold braid, spangled quills, and calla lilies. She carried a secret heartache through the worried fortnight of Victoria's illness, and the busy days that followed; for Mrs. Carr-Boldt had one of many nervous break-downs, and took her turn at the hospital when Victoria came home. For the first time in five happy years, Margaret drooped, and for the first time a longing for money and power of her own gnawed at the girl's heart. If she had but her share of these things, she could hold her own against a hundred Maude and Lily Allens.

As it was, she told herself a little bitterly, she was only a secretary, one of the hundred paid dependents of a rich woman. She was only, after all, a little middle-class country school teacher.

CHAPTER V

"So you're going home to your own people for the week end, Peggy?—And how many of you are there,—I always forget?" said young Mrs. George Crawford, negligently. She tipped back in her chair, half shut her novel, half shut her eyes, and looked critically at her finger-nails.

Outside the big country house summer sunshine flooded the smooth lawns, sparkled on the falling diamonds and still pool of the fountain, glowed over acres of matchless wood and garden. But deep awnings made a clear cool shade indoors, and the wide rooms were delightfully breezy.

Margaret, busy with a ledger and cheque-book, smiled absently, finished a long column, made an orderly entry, and wiped her pen.

"Seven," said she, smiling.

"Seven!" echoed Mrs. Potter, lazily. "My heaven—seven children! How early Victorian!"

"Isn't it?" said a third woman, a very beautiful woman, Mrs. Watts Watson, who was also idling and reading in the white-and-gray morning room. "Well," she added, dropping her magazine, and locking her hands about her head, "my grandmother had ten. Fancy trying to raise ten children!"

"Oh, everything's different now," the first speaker said indifferently. "Everything's more expensive, life is more complicated. People used to have roomier houses, aunts and cousins and grandmothers living with them; there was always some one at home with the children. Nowadays we don't do that."

"And thank the saints we don't!" said Mrs. Watson, piously. "If there's one thing I can't stand, it's a houseful of things-in-law!"

"Of course; but I mean it made the family problem simpler," Mrs. Crawford pursued. "Oh—and I don't know! Everything was so simple. All this business of sterilizing, and fumigating, and pasteurizing, and vaccinating, and boiling in boracic acid wasn't done in those days," she finished vaguely.

"Now there you are—now there you are!" said Mrs. Carr-Boldt, entering into the conversation with sudden force. Entirely recovered after her nervous collapse, as brisk as ever in her crisp linen gown, she was signing the cheques that Margaret handed her, frowningly busy and absorbed with her accounts. Now she leaned back in her chair, glanced at the watch at her wrist, and relaxed the cramped muscles of her body. "That's exactly it, Rose," said she to Mrs. Crawford. "Life is more complicated. People—the very people who ought to have children— simply cannot afford it! And who's to blame? Can you blame a woman whose life is packed full of other things she simply cannot avoid, if she declines to complicate things any further? Our grandmothers didn't have telephones, or motor-cars, or week-end affairs, or even—for that matter—manicures and hair-dressers! A good heavy silk was full dress all the year 'round. They washed their own hair. The 'up-stairs girl' answered the doorbell,—why, they didn't even have talcum powder and nursery refrigerators, and sanitary rugs that have to be washed every day! Do you suppose my grandmother ever took a baby's temperature, or had its eyes and nose examined, or its adenoids cut? They had more children, and they lost more children,—without any reason or logic whatever. Poor things, they never thought of doing anything else, I suppose! A fat old darky nurse brought up the whole crowd—it makes one shudder to think of it! Why, I had always a trained nurse, and the regular nurse used to take two baths a day. I insisted on that, and both nurseries were washed out every day with chloride of potash solution, and the iron beds washed every week! And even then Vic had this mastoid trouble, and Harriet got everything, almost."

"Exactly," said Mrs. Watson. "That's you, Hattie, with all the money in the world. Now do you wonder that some of the rest of us, who have to think of money—in short," she finished decidedly, "do you wonder that people are not having children? At first, naturally, one doesn't want them,—for three or four years, I'm sure, the thought doesn't come into one's head. But then, afterwards,—you see, I've been married fifteen years now!—afterwards, I think it would be awfully nice to have one or two little kiddies, if it was a possible thing. But it isn't."

"No, it isn't," Mrs. Crawford agreed. "You don't want to have them unless you're able to do everything in the world for them. If I were Hat here, I'd have a dozen."

"Oh, no, you wouldn't," Mrs. Carr-Boldt assured her promptly. "No, you wouldn't! You can't leave everything to servants—there are clothes to think of, and dentists, and special teachers, and it's frightfully hard to get a nursery governess. And then you've got to see that they know the right people—don't you know?—and give them parties—I tell you it's a strain."

"Well, I don't believe my mother with her seven ever worked any harder than you do!" said Margaret, with the admiration in her eyes that was so sweet to the older woman. "Look at this morning—did you sit down before you came in here twenty minutes ago?"

"I? Indeed I didn't!" Mrs. Carr-Boldt said. "I had my breakfast and letters at seven, bath at eight, straightened out that squabble between Swann and the cook,—I think Paul is still simmering, but that's neither here nor there!—then I went down with the vet to see the mare. Joe'll never forgive me if I've really broken the creature's knees!—then I telephoned mother, and saw Harriet's violin man, and talked to that Italian Joe sent up to clean the oils,—he's in the gallery now, and—let's see—"

"Italian lesson," Margaret prompted.

"Italian lesson," the other echoed, "and then came in here to sign my cheques."

"You're so executive, Harriet!" said Mrs. Crawford, languidly.

"Apropos of Swann," Margaret said, "he confided to me that he has seven children—on a little farm down on Long Island."

"The butler—oh, I dare say!" Mrs. Watson agreed. "They can, because they've no standard to maintain—seven, or seventeen— the only difference in expense is the actual amount of bread and butter consumed."

"It's too bad," said Mrs. Crawford. "But you've got to handle the question sanely and reasonably, like any other. Now, I love children," she went on. "I'm perfectly crazy about my sister's little girl. She's eleven now, and the cutest thing alive. But when I think of all Mabel's been through, since she was born,—I realize that it's a little too much to expect of any woman. Now, look at us,—there are thousands of people fixed as we are. We're in an apartment hotel, with one maid. There's no room for a second maid, no porch and no back yard. Well, the baby comes,—one loses, before and after the event, just about six months of everything, and of course the expense is frightful, but no matter!—the baby comes. We take a house. That means three indoor maids, George's chauffeur, a man for lawn and furnace- that's five—"

"Doubling expenses," said Mrs. Carr-Boldt, thoughtfully.

"Doubling—! Trebling, or more. But that's not all. Baby must be out from eleven to three every day. So you've got to go sit by the carriage in the park while nurse goes home for her lunch. Or, if you're out for luncheon, or giving a luncheon, she brings baby home, bumps the carriage into the basement, carries the baby upstairs, eats her lunch in snatches—the maids don't like it, and I don't blame them! I know how it was with Mabel; she had to give up that wonderful old apartment of theirs on Gramercy Park. Sid had his studio on the top floor, and she had such a lovely flat on the next floor, but there was no lift, and no laundry, and the kitchen was small—a baby takes so much fussing! And then she lost that splendid cook of hers, Germaine. She wouldn't stand it. Up to that time she'd been cooking and waiting, too, but the baby ended that. Mabel took a house, and Sid paid studio rent beside, and they had two maids, and then three maids,—and what with their fighting, and their days off, and eternally changing, Mabel was a wreck. I've seen her trying to play a bridge hand with Dorothy bobbing about on her arm—poor girl! Finally they went to a hotel, and of course the child got older, and was less trouble. But to this day Mabel doesn't dare leave her alone for one second. And when they go out to dinner, and leave her alone in the hotel, of course the child cries—!"

"That's the worst of a kiddie," Mrs. Watson said. "You can't ever turn 'em off, as it were, or make it spades! They're always right on the job.

I'll never forget Elsie Clay. She was the best friend I had,—my brides-maid, too. She married, and after a while they took a house in Jersey because of the baby. I went out there to lunch one day. There she was in a house perfectly buried in trees, with the rain sopping down out-side, and smoke blowing out of the fireplace, and the drawing-room as dark as pitch at two o'clock. Elsie said she used to nearly die of loneliness, sitting there all afternoon long listening to the trains whistling, and the maid thumping irons in the kitchen, and picking up the baby's blocks. And they quarrelled, you know, she and her husband—that was the beginning of the trouble. Finally the boy went to his grandmother, and now believe Elsie's married again, and living in California somewhere."

Margaret, hanging over the back of her chair, was an attentive listener.

"But people—people in town have children!" she said. "The Blankenships have one, and haven't the de Normandys?"

"The Blankenship boy is in college," said Mrs. Carr-Boldt; "and the little de Normandys lived with their grandmother until they were old enough for boarding school."

"Well, the Deanes have three!" Margaret said triumphantly.

"Ah, well, my dear! Harry Deane's a rich man, and she was a Pell of Philadelphia," Mrs. Crawford supplied promptly. "Now the Eastmans have three, too, with a trained nurse apiece."

"I see," Margaret admitted slowly.

"Far wiser to have none at all," said Mrs. Carr-Boldt, in her decisive way, "than to handicap them from the start by letting them see other children enjoying pleasures and advantages they can't afford. And now, girls, let's stop wasting time. It's half-past eleven. Why can't we have a game of auction right here and now?"

Margaret returned to her cheque-book with speed. The other two, glad to be aroused, heartily approved the idea.

"Well, what does this very businesslike aspect imply?" Mrs. Carr-Boldt asked her secretary.

"It means that I can't play cards, and you oughtn't," Margaret said, laughing.

"Oh—? Why not?"

"Because you've lots of things to do, and I've got to finish these notes, and I have to sit with Harriet while she does her German—"

"Where's Fraulein?"

"Fraulein's going to drive Vic over to the Partridges' for luncheon, and I promised Swann I'd talk to him about favors and things for tomorrow night."

"Well—busy Lizzie! And what have I to do?"

Margaret reached for a well-filled date-book.

"You were to decide about those alterations, the porch and dining room, you know," said she. "There are some architect's sketches around here; the man's going to be here early in the morning. You said you'd drive to the yacht club, to see about the stage for the children's play; you were to stop on the way back and see old Mrs. McNab a moment. You wanted to write Mrs. Polk a note to catch the 'Kaiserin Augusta', and luncheon's early because of the Kellogg bridge." She shut the book. "And call Mr. Carr-Boldt at the club at one," she added.

"All that, now fancy!" said her employer, admiringly.

She had swept some scattered magazines from a small table, and was now seated there, negligently shuffling a pack of cards in her fine white hands.

"Ring, will you, Peggy?" said she.

"And the boat races are to-day, and you dine at Oaks-in-the-Field," Margaret supplemented inflexibly.

"Yes? Well, come and beat the seven of clubs," said Mrs. Carr-Boldt, spreading the deck for the draw.

"Fraulein," she said sweetly, a moment later, when a maid had summoned that worthy and earnest governess, "tell Miss Harriet that Mother doesn't want her to do her German to-day, it's too warm. Tell her that she's to go with you and Miss Victoria for a drive. Thank you. And, Fraulein, will you telephone old Mrs. McNab, and say that Mrs. Carr Boldt is lying down with a severe headache, and she won't be able to come in this morning? Thank you. And, Fraulein, telephone the yacht club, will you? And tell Mr. Mathews that Mrs. Carr-Boldt is indisposed and he'll have to come back this afternoon. I'll talk to him before the children's races. And—one thing more! Will you tell Swann Miss Paget will see him about to-morrow's dinner when she comes back from the yacht club to-day? And tell him to send us something cool to drink now. Thank you so much. No, shut it. Thank you. Have a nice drive!"

They all drew up their chairs to the table.

"You and I, Rose," said Mrs. Watson. "I'm so glad you suggested this, Hattie. I am dying to play."

"It really rests me more than anything else," said Mrs. Carr-Boldt. "Two spades."

CHAPTER VI

Archerton, a blur of flying trees and houses, bright in the late sunlight, Pottsville, with children wading and shouting, under the
bridge, Hunt's Crossing, then the next would be Weston—and
home.

Margaret, beginning to gather wraps and small possessions together,
sighed. She sighed partly because her head ached, partly because the
hot trip had mussed her usual fresh trimness, largely because she was
going home.

This was August; her last trip home had been between Christmas and
the New Year. She had sent a box from Germany at Easter, ties for
the boys, silk scarves for Rebecca, books for Dad; and she had written Mother for her birthday in June, and enclosed an exquisite bit of
lace in the letter; but although Victoria's illness had brought her to
America nearly three months ago, it had somehow been impossible,
she wrote them, to come home until now. Margaret had paid a great
deal for the lace, as a sort of salve for her conscience,—not that
Mother would ever wear it!

Here was Weston. Weston looking its very ugliest in the level pitiless rays of the afternoon sun. The town, like most of its inhabitants, was wilted and grimed after the burden and heat of the long summer day. Margaret carried her heavy suit-case slowly up Main Street. Shop windows were spotted and dusty, and shopkeepers, standing idle in their doorways, looked spotted and dusty too. A cloud of flies fought and surged about the closely guarded door of the butcher shop; a delivery cart was at the curb, the discouraged horse switching an ineffectual tail.

As Margaret passed this cart, a tall boy of fourteen came out of the shop with a bang of the wire-netting door, and slid a basket into the back of the cart.

"Teddy!" said Margaret, irritation evident in her voice, in spite of herself.

"Hello, Mark!" said her brother, delightedly. "Say, great to see you! Get in on the four-ten?"

"Ted," said Margaret, kissing him, as the Pagets always quite simply kissed each other when they met, "what are you driving Costello's cart for?"

"Like to," said Theodore, simply. "Mother doesn't care. Say, you look swell, Mark!"

"What makes you want to drive this horrid cart, Ted?" protested Margaret. "What does Costello pay you?"

"Pay me?" scowled her brother, gathering up the reins. "Oh, come out of it, Marg'ret! He doesn't pay me anything. Don't you make Mother stop me, either, will you?" he ended anxiously.

"Of course I won't!" Margaret said impatiently.

"Giddap, Ruth!" said Theodore; but departing, he pulled up to add cheerfully, "Say, Dad didn't get his raise."

"Did?" said Margaret, brightening.

"Didn't!" He grinned affectionately upon her as with a dislocating jerk the cart started a ricochetting career down the street, with that abandon known only to butchers' carts. Margaret, changing her heavy suit-case to the rested arm, was still vexedly watching it, when two girls, laughing in the open doorway of the express company's office across the street, caught sight of her. One of them, a little vision of pink hat and ruffles, and dark eyes and hair, came running to join her.

Rebecca was now sixteen, and of all the handsome Pagets the best to look upon. She was dressed according to her youthful lights; every separate article of her apparel to-day, from her rowdyish little hat to her openwork hose, represented a battle with Mrs. Paget's preconceived ideas as to propriety in dress, with the honors largely for Rebecca. Rebecca had grown up, in eight months, her sister thought, confusedly; she was no longer the adorable, un-self-conscious tomboy who fought and skated and toboganned with the boys.

"Hello, darling dear!" said Rebecca. "Too bad no one met you! We all thought you were coming on the six. Crazy about your suit! Here's Maudie Pratt. You know Maudie, don't you, Mark?"

Margaret knew Maudie. Rebecca's infatuation for plain, heavy-featured, complacent Miss Pratt was a standing mystery in the Paget family. Margaret smiled, bowed.

"I think we stumbled upon a pretty little secret of yours to-day, Miss Margaret," said Maudie, with her best company manner, as they walked along. Margaret raised her eyebrows. "Rebel and I," Maudie went on,- Rebecca was at the age that seeks a piquant substitute for an unpoetical family name,—"Rebel and I are wondering if we may ask you who Mr. John Tenison is?"

John Tenison! Margaret's heart stood still with a shock almost sickening, then beat furiously. What—how—who on earth had told them anything of John Tenison? Coloring high, she looked sharply at Rebecca.

"Cheer up, angel," said Rebecca, "he's not dead. He sent a telegram to-day, and Mother opened it—"

"Naturally," said Margaret, concealing an agony of impatience, as Rebecca paused apologetically.

"He's with his aunt, at Dayton, up the road here," continued Rebecca; "and wants you to wire him if he may come down and spend tomorrow here."

Margaret drew a relieved breath. There was time to turn around, at least.

"Who is he, sis?" asked Rebecca.

"Why, he's an awfully clever professor, honey," Margaret answered serenely. "We heard him lecture in Germany this spring, and met him afterwards. I liked him very much. He's tremendously interesting." She tried to keep out of her voice the thrill that shook her at the mere thought of him. Confused pain and pleasure stirred her to the very heart.—He wanted to come to see her, he must have telephoned Mrs. Carr-Boldt and asked to call, or he would not have known that she was at home this week end,—surely that was significant, surely that meant something! The thought was all pleasure, so great a joy and pride indeed that Margaret was conscious of wanting to lay it aside, to think of, dream of, ponder over, when she was alone. But, on the other hand, there was instantly the miserable conviction that he mustn't be allowed to come to Weston, no—no—she couldn't have him see her home and her people on a crowded hot summer Sunday, when the town looked its ugliest, and the children were home from school, and when the scramble to get to church and to safely accomplish the one o'clock dinner exhausted the women of the family. And how could she keep him from coming, what excuse could she give?

"Don't you want him to come—is he old and fussy?" asked Rebecca, interestedly.

"I'll see," Margaret answered vaguely. "No, he's only thirty-two or four."

"And charming!" said Maudie archly. Margaret eyed her with a coolness worthy of Mrs. Carr-Boldt herself, and then turned rather pointedly to Rebecca.

"How's Mother, Becky?"

"Oh, she's fine!" Rebecca said, absently in her turn. When Maudie left them at the next corner, she said quickly:—

"Mark, did you see where we were when I saw you?"

"At the express office—? Yes," Margaret said, surprised.

"Well, listen," said Rebecca, reddening. "Don't say anything to Mother about it, will you? She thinks those boys are fresh in there— She don't like me to go in!"

"Oh, Beck—then you oughtn't!" Margaret protested.

"Well, I wasn't!" Rebecca said uncomfortably. "We went to see if Maudie's racket had come. You won't—will you, Mark?"

"Tell Mother—no, I won't," Margaret said, with a long sigh. She looked sideways at Rebecca,—the dainty, fast-forming little figure, the even ripple and curl of her plaited hair, the assured pose of the pretty head. Victoria Carr-Boldt, just Rebecca's age, as a big school-girl still, self-conscious and inarticulate, her well-groomed hair in an unbecoming "club," her well-hung skirts unbecomingly short. Margaret had half expected to find Rebecca at the same stage of development.

Rebecca was cheerful now, the promise exacted, and cheerfully observed:—

"Dad didn't get his raise—isn't that the limit?"

Margaret sighed again, shrugged wearily. They were in their own quiet side street now, a street lined with ugly, shabby houses and beautified by magnificent old elms and maples. The Pagets' own particular gate was weather-peeled, the lawn trampled and bare. A bulging wire netting door gave on the shabby old hall Margaret knew so well; she went on into the familiar rooms, acutely conscious, as she always was for the first hour or two at home, of the bareness and ugliness everywhere—the old sofa that sagged in the seat, the scratched rockers, the bookcases overflowing with coverless magazines, and the old square piano half-buried under loose sheets of music.

Duncan sat on the piano bench—gloomily sawing at a violoncello. Robert,—nine now, with all his pretty baby roundness gone, a lean little burned, peeling face, and big teeth missing when he smiled, stood in the bay window, twisting the already limp net curtains into a tight rope. Each boy gave Margaret a kiss that seemed curiously to taste of dust, sunburn, and freckles, before she followed a noise of hissing and voices to the kitchen to find Mother.

The kitchen, at five o'clock on Saturday afternoon, was in wild confusion, and insufferably hot. Margaret had a distinct impression that
not a movable article therein was in place, and not an available inch
of tables or chairs unused, before her eyes reached the tall figure of
the woman in a gown of chocolate percale, who was frying cutlets at
the big littered range. Her face was dark with heat, and streaked with
perspiration. She turned as Margaret entered, and gave a delighted
cry.

"Well, there's my girl! Bless her heart! Look out for this spoon, lovey,"
she added immediately, giving the girl a guarded embrace. Tears of
joy stood frankly in her fine eyes.

"I meant to have all of this out of the way, dear," apologized Mrs.
Paget, with a gesture that included cakes in the process of frosting,
salad vegetables in the process of cooling, soup in the process of getting strained, great loaves of bread that sent a delicious fragrance over
all the other odors. "But we didn't look for you until six."

"Oh, no matter!" Margaret said bravely.

"Rebecca tell you Dad didn't get his raise?" called Mrs. Paget, in a
voice that rose above the various noises of the kitchen. "Blanche!" she
protested, "can't that wait?" for the old negress had begun to crack ice
with deafening smashes. But Blanche did not hear, so Mrs. Paget
continued loudly: "Dad saw Redman himself; he'll tell you about it!
Don't stay in the kitchen in that pretty dress, dear! I'm coming right
upstairs."

It was very hot upstairs; the bedrooms smelled faintly of matting, the
soap in the bathroom was shrivelled in its saucer. In Margaret's old
room the week's washing had been piled high on the bed. She took
off her hat and linen coat, brushed her hair back from her face, fling-
ing her head back and shutting her eyes the better to fight tears, as
she did so, and began to assort the collars and shirts and put them

away. For Dad's bureau—for Bruce's bureau—for the boys' bureau, table cloths to go downstairs, towels for the shelves in the bathroom. Two little shirtwaists for Rebecca with little holes torn through them where collar and belt pins belonged.

Her last journey took her to the big, third-story room where the three younger boys slept. The three narrow beds were still unmade, and the western sunlight poured over tumbled blankets and the scattered small possessions that seem to ooze from the pores of little boys, Margaret set her lips distastefully as she brought order out of chaos. It was all wrong, somehow, she thought, gathering handkerchiefs and matches and "Nick Carters" and the oiled paper that had wrapped caramels from under the pillows that would in a few hours harbor a fresh supply.

She went out on the porch in time to put her arms about her father's shabby shoulders when he came in. Mr. Paget was tired, and he told his wife and daughters that he thought he was a very sick man. Margaret's mother met this statement with an anxious solicitude that was very soothing to the sufferer. She made Mark get Daddy his slippers and loose coat, and suggested that Rebecca shake up the dining-room couch before she established him there, in a rampart of pillows. No outsider would have dreamed that Mrs. Paget had dealt with this exact emergency some hundreds of times in the past twenty years.

Mr. Paget, reclining, shut his eyes, remarked that he had had an "awful, awful day," and wondered faintly if it would be too much trouble to have "somebody" make him just a little milk toast for his dinner. He smiled at Margaret when she sat down beside him; all the children were dear, but the oldest daughter knew she came first with her father.

"Getting to be an old, old man!" he said wearily, and Margaret hated herself because she had to quell an impatient impulse to tell him he was merely tired and cross and hungry, before she could say, in the proper soothing tone, "Don't talk that way, Dad darling!" She had to listen to a long account of the "raise," wincing every time her father emphasized the difference between her own position and that of her employer. Dad was at least the equal of any one in Weston! Why, a man Dad's age oughtn't to be humbly asking a raise, he ought to be dictating now. It was just Dad's way of looking at things, and it was all wrong.

"Well, I'll tell you one thing!" said Rebecca, who had come in with a brimming soup plate of milk toast, "Joe Redman gave a picnic last month, and he came here with his mother, in the car, to ask me. And I was the scornfullest thing you ever saw, wasn't I, Ted? Not much!"

"Oh, Beck, you oughtn't to mix social and business things that way!" Margaret said helplessly.

"Dinner!" screamed the nine-year-old Robert, breaking into the room at this point, and "Dinner!" said Mrs. Paget, wearily, cheerfully, from the chair into which she had dropped at the head of the table. Mr. Paget, revived by sympathy, milk toast, and Rebecca's attentions, took his place at the foot, and Bruce the chair between Margaret and his mother. Like the younger boys, whose almost confluent freckles had been brought into unusual prominence by violently applied soap and water, and whose hair dripped on their collars, he had brushed up for dinner, but his negligee shirt and corduroy trousers were stained and spotted from machine oil. Margaret, comparing him secretly to the men she knew, as daintily groomed as women, in their spotless white, felt a little resentment that Bruce's tired face was so contented, and said to herself again that it was all wrong.

Dinner was the same old haphazard meal with which she was so familiar; Blanche supplying an occasional reproof to the boys, Ted ignoring his vegetables, and ready in an incredibly short time for a second cutlet, and Robert begging for corn syrup, immediately after the soup, and spilling it from his bread. Mrs. Paget was flushed, her disappearances kitchenward frequent. She wanted Margaret to tell her all about Mr. Tenison. Margaret laughed, and said there was nothing to tell.

"You might get a horse and buggy from Peterson's," suggested Mrs. Paget, interestedly, "and drive about after dinner."

"Oh, Mother, I don't think I had better let him come!" Margaret said. "There's so many of us, and such confusion, on Sunday! Ju and Harry are almost sure to come over."

"Yes, I guess they will," Mrs. Paget said, with her sudden radiant smile. "Ju is so dear in her little house, and Harry's so sweet with her," she went on with vivacity. "Daddy and I had dinner with them Tuesday. Bruce said Rebecca was lovely with the boys,—we're going to Julie's again sometime. I declare it's so long since we've been any-where without the children that we both felt funny. It was a lovely evening."

"You're too much tied, Mother," Margaret said affectionately.

"Not now!" her mother protested radiantly. "With all my babies turning into men and women so fast. And I'll have you all together to-morrow- and your friend I hope, too, Mark," she added hos-pitably. "You had better let him come, dear. There's a big dinner, and I always freeze more cream than we need, anyway, because Daddy likes a plate of it about four o'clock, if there's any left."

"Well—but there's nothing to do," Margaret protested.

"No, but dinner takes quite a while," Mrs. Paget suggested a little doubtfully; "and we could have a nice talk on the porch, and then you could go driving or walking. I wish there was something cool and pleasant to do, Mark," she finished a little wistfully. "You do just as you think best about asking him to come."

"I think I'll wire him that another time would be better," said Margaret, slowly. "Sometime we'll regularly arrange for it."

"Well, perhaps that would be best," her mother agreed. "Some other time we'll send the boys off before dinner, and have things all nice and quiet. In October, say, when the trees are so pretty. I don't know but what that's my favorite time of all the year!"

Margaret looked at her as if she found something new in the tired, bright face. She could not understand why her mother—still too heated to commence eating her dinner—should radiate so definite an atmosphere of content, as she sat back a little breathless, after the flurry of serving. She herself felt injured and sore, not at the mere disappointment it caused her to put off John Tendon's visit, but because she felt more acutely than ever to-night the difference between his position and her own.

"Something nice has happened, Mother?" she hazarded, entering with an effort into the older woman's mood.

"Nothing special." Her mother's happy eyes ranged about the circle of young faces. "But it's so lovely to have you here, and to have Ju coming to-morrow," she said. "I just wish Daddy could build a house for each one of you, as you marry and settle down, right around our house in a circle, as they say people do sometimes in the Old World. I think then I'd have nothing in life to wish for!"

"Oh, Mother—in Weston!" Margaret said hopelessly, but her mother did not catch it.

"Not, Mark," she went on hastily and earnestly, "that I'm not more than grateful to God for all His goodness, as it is! I look at other women, and I wonder, I wonder—what I have done to be so blessed! Mark—" her face suddenly glowed, she leaned a little toward her daughter, "dearie, I must tell you," she said; "it's about Ju—"

Their eyes met in the pause.

"Mother—really?" Margaret said slowly.

"She told me on Tuesday,." Mrs. Paget said, with glistening eyes. "Now, not a word to any one, Mark,—but she'll want you to know!"

"And is she glad?" Margaret said, unable to rejoice.

"Glad?" Mrs. Paget echoed, her face gladness itself.

"Well, Ju's so young,—just twenty-one," Margaret submitted a little uncertainly; "and she's been so free,—and they're just in the new house! And I thought they were going to Europe!"

"Oh, Europe!" Mrs. Paget dismissed it cheerfully. "Why, it's the happiest time in a woman's life, Mark! Or I don't know, though," she went on thoughtfully,—"I don't know but what I was happiest when you were all tiny, tumbling about me, and climbing into my lap.... Why, you love children, dear," she finished, with a shade of reproach in her voice, as Margaret still looked sober.

"Yes, I know, Mother," Margaret said. "But Julie's only got the one maid, and I don't suppose they can have another. I hope to goodness Ju won't get herself all run down!"

Her mother laughed. "You remind me of Grandma Paget," said she, cheerfully; "she lived ten miles away when we were married, but she came in when Bruce was born. She was rather a proud, cold woman herself, but she was very sweet to me. Well, then little Charlie came, fourteen months later, and she took that very seriously. Mother was dead, you know, and she stayed with me again, and worried me half sick telling me that it wasn't fair to Bruce and it wasn't fair to Charlie to divide my time between them that way. Well, then when my third baby was coming, I didn't dare tell her. Dad kept telling me to, and I couldn't, because I knew what a calamity a third would seem to her! Finally she went to visit Aunt Rebecca out West, and it was the very day she got back that the baby came. She came upstairs—she'd come right up from the train, and not seen any one but Dad; and he wasn't very intelligible, I guess—and she sat down and took the baby in her arms, and says she, looking at me sort of patiently, yet as if she was exasperated too: 'Well, this is a nice way to do, the minute my back's turned! What are you going to call him, Julia?' And I said, 'I'm going to call her Margaret, for my dear husband's mother, and she's going to be beautiful and good, and grow up to marry the President!'" Mrs. Paget's merry laugh rang out. "I never shall forget your grandmother's face."

"Just the same," Mrs. Paget added, with a sudden deep sigh, "when little Charlie left us, the next year, and Brucie and Dad were both so ill, she and I agreed that you—you were just talking and trying to walk—were the only comfort we had! I could wish my girls no greater happiness than my children have been to me," finished Mother, contentedly.

"I know," Margaret began, half angrily; "but what about the children?" she was going to add. But somehow the arguments she had used so plausibly did not utter themselves easily to Mother, whose children would carry into their own middle age a wholesome dread of her anger. Margaret faltered, and merely scowled.

"I don't like to see that expression on your face, dearie," her mother said, as she might have said it to an eight-year-old child. "Be my sweet girl! Why, marriage isn't marriage without children, Mark. I've been thinking all week of having a baby in my arms again,—it's so long since Rob was a baby."

Margaret devoted herself, with a rather sullen face, to her dessert. Mother would never feel as she did about these things, and what was the use of arguing? In the silence she heard her father speak loudly and suddenly.

"I am not in a position to have my children squander money on concerts and candy," he said. Margaret forgot her own grievance, and looked up. The boys looked resentful and gloomy; Rebecca was flushed, her eyes dropped, her lips trembling with disappointment.

"I had promised to take them to the Elks Concert and dance," Mrs. Paget interpreted hastily. "But now Dad says the Bakers are coming over to play whist."

"Is it going to be a good show, Ted?" Margaret asked.

"Oh," Rebecca flashed into instant glowing response. "It's going to be a dandy! Every one's going to be there! Ford Patterson is going to do a monologue,—he's as good as a professional!—and George is going to send up a bunch of carrots and parsnips! And the Weston Male Quartette, Mark, and a playlet by the Hunt's Crossing Amateur Theatrical Society!"

"Oh—oh!"—Margaret mimicked the eager rush of words. "Let me take them, Dad," she pleaded, "if it's going to be as fine as all that! I'll stand treat for the crowd."

"Oh, Mark, you darling!" burst from the rapturous Rebecca.

"Say, gee, we've got to get there early!" Theodore warned them, finishing his pudding with one mammoth spoonful.

"If you take them, my dear," Mr. Paget said graciously, "of course Mother and I are quite satisfied."

"I'll hold Robert by one ear and Rebecca by another," Margaret promised; "and if she so much as dares to look at George or Ted or Jimmy Barr or Paul, I'll—"

"Oh, Jimmy belongs to Louise, now," said Rebecca, radiantly. There was a joyous shout of laughter from the light-hearted juniors, and Rebecca, seeing her artless admission too late, turned scarlet while she laughed. Dinner broke up in confusion, as dinner at home always did, and everybody straggled upstairs to dress.

Margaret, changing her dress in a room that was insufferably hot, because the shades must be down, and the gas-lights as high as possible, reflected that another forty-eight hours would see her speeding back to the world of cool, awninged interiors, uniformed maids, the clink of iced glasses, the flash of white sails on blue water. She could surely afford for that time to be patient and sweet. She lifted Rebecca's starched petticoat from the bed to give Mother a seat, when Mother came rather wearily in to watch them.

"Sweet girl to take them, Mark," said Mother, appreciatively. "I was going to ask Brucie. But he's gone to bed, poor fellow; he's worn out to-night."

"He had a letter from Ned Gunther this morning," said Rebecca, cheerfully,—powdering the tip of her pretty nose, her eyes almost crossed with concentration,—"and I think it made him blue all day."

"Ned Gunther?" said Margaret.

"Chum at college," Rebecca elucidated; "a lot of them are going to Honolulu, just for this month, and of course they wanted Bruce. Mark, does that show?"

Margaret's heart ached for the beloved brother's disappointment. There it was again, all wrong! Before she left the house with the rioting youngsters, she ran upstairs to his room. Bruce, surrounded by scientific magazines, a drop-light with a vivid green shade over his shoulder, looked up with a welcoming smile.

"Sit down and talk, Mark," said he.

Margaret explained her hurry.

"Bruce,—this isn't much fun!" she said, looking about the room with its shabby dresser and worn carpet. "Why aren't you going to the concert?"

"Is there a concert?" he asked, surprised.

"Why, didn't you hear us talking at dinner? The Elks, you know."

"Well—sure! I meant to go to that. I forgot it was to-night," he said, with his lazy smile. "I came home all in, forgot everything."

"Oh, come,!" Margaret urged, as eagerly as Rebecca ever did. "It's early, Bruce, come on! You don't have to shave! We'll hold a seat,—come on!"

"Sure, I will!" he said, suddenly roused. The magazines rapped on the floor, and Margaret had barely shut the door behind her when she heard his bare feet follow them.

It was like old times to sit next to him through the hot merry evening, while Rebecca glowed like a little rose among her friends, and the smaller boys tickled her ear with their whispered comments. Margaret had sent a telegram to Professor Tenison, and felt relieved that at least that strain was spared her. She even danced with Bruce after the concert, and with one or two old friends.

Afterwards, they strolled back slowly through the inky summer dark, finding the house hot and close when they came in. Margaret went upstairs, hearing her mother's apologetic, "Oh, Dad, why didn't I give you back your club?" as she passed the dining-room door. She knew Mother hated whist, and wondered rather irritably why she played it. The Paget family was slow to settle down. Robert became tearful and whining before he was finally bumped protesting into bed. Theodore and Duncan prolonged their ablutions until the noise of shouting, splashing, and thumping in the bathroom brought Mother to the foot of the stairs. Rebecca was conversational. She lay with her slender arms locked behind her head on the pillow, and talked, as Julie had talked on that memorable night five years ago. Margaret, restless in the hot darkness, wondering whether the maddening little shaft of light from the hall gas was annoying enough to warrant the effort of getting up and extinguishing it, listened and listened.

Rebecca wanted to join the Stage Club, but Mother wouldn't let her unless Bruce did. Rebecca belonged to the Progressive Diners. Did Mark suppose Mother'd think she was crazy if she asked the family not to be in evidence when the crowd came to the house for the salad course? And Rebecca wanted to write to Bruce's chum, not regularly, you know, Mark, but just now and then, he was so nice! And Mother didn't like the idea. Margaret was obviously supposed to lend a hand with these interesting tangles.

"...and I said, 'Certainly not! I won't unmask at all, if it comes to that!'... And imagine that elegant fellow carrying my old books and my skates! So I wrote, and Maudie and I decided... And Mark, if it wasn't a perfectly gorgeous box of roses!... That old, old dimity, but Mother pressed and freshened it up.... Not that I want to marry him, or any one..."

Margaret wakened from uneasy drowsing with a start. The hall was dark now, the room cooler. Rebecca was asleep. Hands, hands she knew well, were drawing a light covering over her shoulders. She opened her eyes to see her mother.

"I've been wondering if you're disappointed about your friend not coming to-morrow, Mark?" said the tender voice.

"Oh, no-o!" said Margaret, hardily. "Mother—why are you up so late?"

"Just going to bed," said the other, soothingly. "Blanche forgot to put the oatmeal into the cooker, and I went downstairs again. I'll say my prayers in here."

Margaret went off to sleep again, as she had so many hundred times before, with her mother kneeling beside her.

CHAPTER VII

It seemed but a few moments before the blazing Sunday was precip-
itated upon them, and everybody was late for everything.

The kitchen was filled with the smoke from hot griddles blue in the
sunshine, when Margaret went downstairs; and in the dining-room
the same merciless light fell upon the sticky syrup pitcher, and upon
the stains on the tablecloth. Cream had been brought in in the bot-
tle, the bread tray was heaped with orange skins, and the rolls piled
on the tablecloth. Bruce, who had already been to church with
Mother, and was off for a day's sail, was dividing his attention
between Robert and his watch. Rebecca, daintily busy with the special cup and plate that were one of her little affectations, was all ready
for the day, except as to dress, wearing a thin little kimono over her
blue ribbons and starched embroideries. Mother was putting up a little lunch for Bruce. Confusion reigned. The younger boys were urged
to hurry, if they wanted to make the "nine." Rebecca was going to
wait for the "half past ten," because the "kids sang at nine, and it was
fierce." Mr. Paget and his sons departed together, and the girls went
upstairs for a hot, tiring tussle with beds and dusting before starting

for church. They left their mother busy with the cream freezer in the kitchen. It was very hot even then.

But it was still hotter, walking home in the burning midday stillness. A group of young people waited lazily for letters, under the trees outside the post-office door. Otherwise the main street was deserted. A languid little breeze brought the far echoes of pianos and phonographs from this direction and that.

"Who's that on the porch?" said Rebecca, suddenly, as they neared home, instantly finding the stranger among her father and the boys. Margaret, glancing up sharply, saw, almost with a sensation of sickness, the big, ungainly figure, the beaming smile, and the shock of dark hair that belonged to nobody else in the world but John Tenison, A stony chill settled about her heart as she went up the steps and gave him her hand.

Oh, if he only couldn't stay to dinner, she prayed. Oh, if only he could spare them time for no more than a flying visit! With a sinking heart she smiled her greetings.

"Doctor Tenison,—this is very nice of you!" Margaret said. "Have you met my father—my small brothers?"

"We have been having a great talk," said John Tenison, genially, "and this young man—" he indicated Robert, "has been showing me the colored supplement of the paper. I didn't have any word from you, Miss Paget," he went on, "so I took the chance of finding you. And your mother has assured me that I will not put her out by staying to have luncheon with you."

"Oh, that's nice!" Margaret said mechanically, trying to dislodge Robert from the most comfortable chair by a significant touch of her fingers on his small shoulder. Robert perfectly understood that she

wanted the chair, but continued in absorbed study of the comic supplement, merely wriggling resentfully at Margaret's touch. Margaret,
at the moment, would have been glad to use violence on the stub-
born, serene little figure. When he was finally dislodged, she sat
down, still flushed from her walk and the nervousness Doctor
Tenison's arrival caused her, and tried to bring the conversation into
a normal channel. But an interruption occurred in the arrival of
Harry and Julie in the runabout; the little boys swarmed down to
examine it. Julie, very pretty, with a perceptible little new air of dig-
nity, went upstairs to freshen hair and gown, and Harry, pushing his
straw hat back the better to mop his forehead, immediately engaged
Doctor Tenison's attention with the details of what sounded to
Margaret like a particularly uninteresting operation, which he had
witnessed the day before.

Utterly discouraged, and acutely wretched, Margaret presently
slipped away, and went into the kitchen, to lend a hand with the dinner reparations if help was needed. The room presented a scene if
possible a little more confused than that of the day before, and was
certainly hotter. Her mother, flushed and hurried, in a fresh but
rather unbecoming gingham, was putting up a cold supper for the
younger boys, who, having duly attended to their religious duties,
were to take a long afternoon tramp, with a possible interval of fish-
ing. She buttered each slice of the great loaf before she cut it, and lifted it carefully on the knife before beginning the next slice. An
opened pot of jam stood at her elbow. A tin cup and the boys' fish-
ing-gear lay on a chair. Theodore and Duncan themselves hung over
these preparations; never apparently helping themselves to food, yet
never with empty mouths. Blanche, moaning "The Palms" with the
insistence of one who wishes to show her entire familiarity with a
melody, was at the range.

Roast veal, instead of the smothered chickens her mother had so
often, and cooked so deliciously, a mountain of mashed potato—

corn on the cob, and an enormous heavy salad mantled with may-onnaise—Margaret could have wept over the hopelessly plebeian dinner!

"Mother, mayn't I get down the finger-bowls," she asked; "and mayn't we have black coffee in the silver pot, afterwards?"

Mrs. Paget looked absently at her for a dubious second. "I don't like to ask Blanche to wash all that extra glass," she said, in an undertone, adding briskly to Theodore, "No, no, Ted! You can't have all that cake. Half that!" and to Blanche herself, "Don't leave the door open when you go in, Blanche; I just drove all the flies out of the dining-room." Then she returned to Margaret with a cordial: "Why, certainly, dear! Any one who wants coffee, after tea, can have it! Dad always wants his cup of tea."

"Nobody but us ever serves tea with dinner!" Margaret muttered; but her mother did not hear it. She buckled the strap of the lunch-box, straightened her back with an air of relief, and pushed down her rolled-up sleeves.

"Don't lose that napkin, Ted," said she, and receiving the boy's grate-ful kiss haphazard between her hair and forehead, she added affec-tionately: "You're more than welcome, dear! We're all ready, Mark,—go and tell them, dear! All right, Blanche."

Ruffled and angry, Margaret went to summon the others to dinner. Maudie had joined them on the porch now, and had been urged to stay, and was already trying her youthful wiles on the professor.

"Well, he'll have to leave on the five o'clock!" Margaret reflected, steeled to bitter endurance until that time. For everything went wrong, and dinner was one long nightmare for her. Professor Tenison's napkin turned out to be a traycloth. Blanche, asked for another, disappeared for several minutes, and returned without it, to whisper in Mrs. Paget's ear. Mrs. Paget immediately sent her own fresh napkin to the guest. The incident, or something in their murmured conversation, gave Rebecca and Maudie "the giggles." There seemed an exhausting amount of passing and repassing of plates. The room was hot, the supply of ice insufficient. Mr. Paget dwelt on his favorite grievance—"the old man isn't needed, these days. They're getting all young fellows into the bank. They put young college fellows in there who are getting pretty near the money I am—after twenty-five years!" In any pause, Mrs. Paget could be heard, patiently dissuading little Robert from his fixed intention of accompanying the older boys on their walk, whether invited or uninvited.

John Tenison behaved charmingly, eating his dinner with enjoyment, looking interestedly from one face to the other, sympathetic, alert, and amused. But Margaret writhed in spirit at what he must be thinking.

Finally the ice cream, in a melting condition, and the chocolate cake, very sticky, made their appearance; and although these were regular Sunday treats, the boys felt called upon to cheer. Julie asked her mother in an audible undertone if she "ought" to eat cake. Doctor Tenison produced an enormous box of chocolates, and Margaret was disgusted with the frantic scramble her brothers made to secure them.

"If you're going for a walk, dear," her mother said, when the meal was over, "you'd better go. It's almost three now."

"I don't know whether we will, it's so hot," Margaret said, in an indifferent tone, but she could easily have broken into disheartened tears.

"Oh, go," Julie urged, "it's much cooler out." They were up in Margaret's old room, Mrs. Paget tying a big apron about Julie's ruffled frock, preparatory to an attack upon the demoralized kitchen. "We think he's lovely," the little matron went on approvingly. "Don't fall in love with him, Mark."

"Why not?" Margaret said carelessly, pinning on her hat.

"Well, I don't imagine he's a marrying man," said the young authority, wisely. Margaret flushed, and was angry at herself for flushing. But when Mrs. Paget had gone downstairs, Julie came very simply and charmingly over to her sister, and standing close beside her with embarrassed eyes on her own hand,—very youthful in its plain ring,— as she played with the bureau furnishing, she said:

"Mother tell you?"

Margaret looked down at the flushed face.

"Are you sorry, Ju?"

"Sorry!" The conscious eyes flashed into view. "Sorry!" Julie echoed in astonishment. "Why, Mark," she said dreamily,—there was no affectation of maturity in her manner now, and it was all the more impressive for that. "Why, Mark," said she, "it's—it's the most wonderful thing that ever happened to me! I think and think,"—her voice dropped very low,—"of holding it in my arms,—mine and Harry's, you know—and of its little face!"

Margaret, stirred, kissed the wet lashes.

"Ju, but you're so young—you're such a baby yourself!" she said.

"And, Mark," Julie said, unheeding, "you know what Harry and I are going to call her, if it's a girl? Not for Mother, for it's so confusing to have two Julias, but for you! Because," her arms went about her sister, "you've always been such a darling to me, Mark!"

Margaret went downstairs very thoughtfully, and out into the silent Sunday streets. Where they walked, or what they talked of, she did not know. She knew that her head ached, and that the village looked very commonplace, and that the day was very hot. She found it more painful than sweet to be strolling along beside the big, loose-jointed figure, and to send an occasional side glance to John Tenison's earnest face, which wore its pleasantest expression now. Ah, well, it would be all over at five o'clock, she said wearily to herself, and she could go home and lie down with her aching head in a darkened room, and try not to think what to-day might have been. Try not to think of the dainty little luncheon Annie would have given them at Mrs. Carr-Boldt's, of the luxurious choice of amusements afterward: motoring over the lovely country roads, rowing on the wide still water, watching the tennis courts, or simply resting in deep chairs on the sweep of velvet lawn above the river.

She came out of a reverie to find Doctor Tenison glancing calmly up from his watch.

"The train was five o'clock, was it?" he said. "I've missed it!"

"Missed it!" Margaret echoed blankly. Then, as the horrible possibility dawned upon her, "Oh, no!"

"Oh, yes,—as bad as that!" he said, laughing at her.

Poor Margaret, fighting despair, struggled to recover herself.

"Well, I thought it might have been important to you!" she said, laughing quite naturally. "There's a seven-six, but it stops everywhere, and a ten-thirty. The ten-thirty is best, because supper's apt to be a little late."

"The ten-thirty," Doctor Tenison echoed contentedly. Margaret's heart sank,—five more hours of the struggle! "But perhaps that's an imposition," he said. "Isn't there a tea-room—isn't there an inn here where we could have a bite?"

"We aren't in Berlin," Margaret reminded him cheerfully. "There's a hotel,—but Mother would never forgive me for leading any one there! No, we'll take that little walk I told you of, and Mother will give us something to eat later.—Perhaps if we're late enough," she added to herself, "we can have just tea and bread and jam alone, after the others."

Suddenly, unreasonably, she felt philosophical and gay. The little episode of missing the train had given her the old dear feeling of adventure and comradeship again. Things couldn't be any worse than they had been at noon, anyway. The experience had been thoroughly disenchanting. What did a few hours, more or less, matter! Let him be disgusted if he wanted to, she couldn't help it!

It was cooler now, the level late shadows were making even Weston pretty. They went up a steep shady lane to the old graveyard, and wandered, peacefully, contentedly, among the old graves. Margaret gathered her thin gown from contact with the tangled, uncut grass; they had to disturb a flock of nibbling sheep to cross to the crumbling wall. Leaning on the uneven stones that formed it, they looked down at the roofs of the village, half lost in tree-tops; and listened to the barking of dogs, and the shrill voices of children. The sun sank lower, lower. There was a feeling of dew in the air as they went slowly home.

When, at seven o'clock, they opened the gate, they found on the side porch only Rebecca, enchanting in something pink and dotted, Mother, and Dad.

"Lucky we waited!" said Rebecca, rising, and signaling some wordless message to Margaret that required dimples, widened eyes, compressed lips, and an expression of utter secrecy. "Supper's all ready," she added casually.

"Where are the others'" Margaret said, experiencing the most pleasant sensation she had had in twenty-four hours.

"Ju and Harry went home, Rob's at George's, boys walking," said Rebecca, briefly, still dimpling mysteriously with additional information. She gave Margaret an eloquent side glance as she led the way into the dining-room. At the doorway Margaret stopped, astounded.

The room was hardly recognizable now. It was cool and delightful, with the diminished table daintily set for five, The old silver candlesticks and silver teapot presided over blue bowls of berries, and the choicest of Mother's preserved fruits. Some one had found time to put fresh parsley about the Canton platter of cold meats, some one had made a special trip to Mrs. O'Brien's for the cream that filled the Wedgwood pitcher. Margaret felt tears press suddenly against her eyes.

"Oh, Beck!" she could only stammer, when the sisters went into the kitchen for hot water and tea biscuit.

"Mother did it," said Rebecca, returning her hug with fervor. "She gave us all an awful talking to, after you left! She said here was dear old Mark, who always worked herself to death for us, trying to make a nice impression, and to have things go smoothly, and we were all acting like Indians, and everything so confused at dinner, and hot and noisy! So, later, when Paul and I and the others were walking, we saw you and Doctor Tenison going up toward the graveyard, and I tore home and told Mother he'd missed the five and would be back; it was after five then, and we just flew!"

It was all like a pleasant awakening after a troubled dream. As Margaret took her place at the little feast, she felt an exquisite sensa-

tion of peace and content sink into her heart. Mother was so gracious
and charming, behind the urn; Rebecca irresistible in her admiration
of the famous professor. Her father was his sweetest self, delightfully
reminiscent of his boyhood, and his visit to the White House in
Lincoln's day, with "my uncle, the judge." But it was to her mother's
face that Margaret's eyes returned most often, she wanted- she was
vaguely conscious that she wanted—to get away from the voices and
laughter, and think about Mother. How sweet she was, just sweet,
and after all, how few people were that in this world! They were
clever, and witty, and rich,—plenty of them, but how little sweetness
there was! How few faces, like her mother's, did not show a line that
was not all tenderness and goodness.

They laughed over their teacups like old friends; the professor and
Rebecca shouting joyously together, Mr. Paget one broad twinkle,
Mrs. Paget radiantly reflecting, as she always did react, the others'
mood. It was a memorably happy hour.

And after tea they sat on the porch, and the stars came out, and
presently the moon sent silver shafts through the dark foliage of the
trees. Little Rob came home, and climbed silently, contentedly, into
his father's lap.

"Sing something, Mark," said Dad, then; and Margaret, sitting on
the steps with her head against her mother's knee, found it very simple to begin in the darkness one of the old songs he loved:—

> "Don't you cry, ma honey,
> Don't you weep no more."

Rebecca, sitting on the rail, one slender arm flung above her head
about the pillar, joined her own young voice to Margaret's sweet and
steady one. The others hummed a little. John Tenison, sitting watching them, his locked hands hanging between his knees, saw in the
moonlight a sudden glitter on the mother's cheek.

Presently Bruce, tired and happy and sunburned, came through the splashed silver-and-black of the street to sit by Margaret, and put his arm about her; and the younger boys, returning full of the day's great deeds, spread themselves comfortably over the lower steps. Before long all their happy voices rose together, on "Believe me," and "Working on the Railroad," and "Seeing Nellie Home," and a dozen more of the old songs that young people have sung for half a century in the summer moonlight.

And then it was time to say good-night to Professor Tenison. "Come again, sir!" said Mr. Paget, heartily; the boys slid their hands, still faintly suggestive of fish, cordially into his; Rebecca promised to mail him a certain discussed variety of fern the very next day; Bruce's voice sounded all hearty good-will as he hoped that he wouldn't miss Doctor Tenison's next visit. Mrs. Paget, her hand in his, raised keen, almost anxious eyes to his face.

"But surely you'll be down our way again?" said she, unsmilingly.

"Oh, surely." The professor was unable to keep his eyes from moving toward Margaret, and the mother saw it.

"Good-bye for the present, then," she said, still very gravely.

"Good-bye, Mrs. Paget," said Doctor Tenison. "It's been an inestimable privilege to meet you all. I haven't ever had a happier day."

Margaret, used to the extravagant speeches of another world, thought this merely very charming politeness. But her heart sang, as they walked away together. He liked them—he had had a nice time!

"Now I know what makes you so different from other women," said John Tenison, when he and Margaret were alone. "It's having that wonderful mother! She—she—well, she's one woman in a million; I don't have to tell you that! It's something to thank God for, a mother like that; it's a privilege to know her. I've been watching her all day, and I've been wondering what she gets out of it,—that was what puzzled me; but now, just now, I've found out! This morning, thinking what her life is, I couldn't see what repaid her, do you see? What made up to her for the unending, unending effort, and sacrifice, the pouring out of love and sympathy and help—year after year after year...."

He hesitated, but Margaret did not speak.

"You know," he went on musingly, "in these days, when women just serenely ignore the question of children, or at most, as a special concession, bring up one or two,—just the one or two whose expenses can be comfortably met!—there's something magnificent in a woman like your mother, who begins eight destinies instead of one! She doesn't strain and chafe to express herself through the medium of poetry or music or the stage, but she puts her whole splendid philosophy into her nursery—launches sound little bodies and minds that have their first growth cleanly and purely about her knees. Responsibility,- that's what these other women say they are afraid of! But it seems to me there's no responsibility like that of decreeing that young lives simply shall not be. Why, what good is learning, or elegance of manner, or painfully acquired fineness of speech, and taste and point of view, if you are not going to distil it into the growing plants, the only real hope we have in the world! You know, Miss Paget," his smile was very sweet, in the half darkness, "there's a higher tribunal than the social tribunal of this world, after all; and it seems to me that a woman who stands there, as your mother will, with a forest of new lives about her, and a record like hers, will—will find she has a Friend at court!" he finished whimsically.

They were at a lonely corner, and a garden fence offering Margaret a convenient support, she laid her arms suddenly upon the rosevine that covered it, and her face upon her arms, and cried as if her heart was broken.

"Why, why—my dear girl!" the professor said, aghast. He laid his hand on the shaking shoulders, but Margaret shook it off.

"I'm not what you think I am!" she sobbed out, incoherently. "I'm not different from other women; I'm just as selfish and bad and mean as the worst of them! And I'm not worthy to t-tie my m-mother's shoes!"

"Margaret!" John Tenison said unsteadily. And in a flash her drooping bright head was close to his lips, and both his big arms were about her. "You know I love you, don't you Margaret?" he said hoarsely, over and over, with a sort of fierce intensity. "You know that, don't you? Don't you, Margaret?"

Margaret could not speak. Emotion swept her like a rising tide from all her familiar moorings; her heart thundered, there was a roaring in her ears. She was conscious of a wild desire to answer him, to say one hundredth part of all she felt; but she could only rest, breathless, against him, her frightened eyes held by the eyes so near, his arms about her.

"You do, don't you, Margaret?" he said more gently. "You love me, don't you? Don't you?"

And after a long time, or what seemed a long time, while they stood motionless in the summer night, with the great branches of the trees moving a little overhead, and garden scents creeping out on the damp air, Margaret said, with a sort of breathless catch in her voice:—

"You know I do!" And with the words the fright left her eyes, and happy tears filled them, and she raised her face to his.

Coming back from the train half an hour later, she walked between a new heaven and a new earth! The friendly stars seemed just overhead; a thousand delicious odors came from garden beds and recently watered lawns. She moved through the confusion that always attended the settling down of the Pagets for the night, like one in a dream, and was glad to find herself at last lying in the darkness beside the sleeping Rebecca again. Now, now, she could think!

But it was all too wonderful for reasonable thought. Margaret clasped both her hands against her rising heart. He loved her. She could think of the very words he had used in telling her, over and over again. She need no longer wonder and dream and despair: he had said it. He loved her, had loved her from the very first. His old aunt suspected it, and his chum suspected it, and he had thought Margaret knew it. And beside him in that brilliant career that she had followed so wistfully in her dreams, Margaret saw herself, his wife. Young and clever and good to look upon,—yes, she was free to-night to admit herself all these good things for his sake!—and his wife, mounting as he mounted beside the one man in the world she had elected to admire and love. "Doctor and Mrs. John Tenison "—so it would be written. "Doctor Tenison's wife"— "This is Mrs. Tenison"—she seemed already to hear the magical sound of it!

Love—what a wonderful thing it was! How good God was to send this best of all gifts to her! She thought how it belittled the other good things of the world. She asked no more of life, now; she was loved by a good man, and a great man, and she was to be his wife. Ah, the happy years together that would date from to-night,— Margaret was thrilling already to their delights. "For better or worse," the old words came to her with a new meaning. There would be no worse, she said to herself with sudden conviction,—how could there be? Poverty, privation, sickness might come,—but to bear them with John,—to comfort and sustain him, to be shut away with him from all the world but the world of their own four walls,—why, that would be the greatest happiness of all! What hardship could be hard that knitted their two hearts closer together; what road too steep if they essayed it hand in hand?

And that—her confused thoughts ran on—that was what had changed all life for Julie. She had forgotten Europe, forgotten all the idle ambitions of her girlhood, because she loved her husband; and now the new miracle was to come to her,—the miracle of a child, the little perfect promise of the days to come. How marvellous—how marvellous it was! The little imperative, helpless third person, bringing to radiant youth and irresponsibility the terrors of danger and anguish, and the great final joy, to share together. That was life. Julie was living; and although Margaret's own heart was not yet a wife's, and she could not yet find room for the love beyond that, still she was strangely, deeply stirred now by a longing for all the experiences that life held.

How she loved everything and everybody to-night,—how she loved just being alive—just being Margaret Paget, lying here in the dark dreaming and thinking. There was no one in the world with whom she would change places to-night! Margaret found herself thinking of one woman of her acquaintance after another,—and her own future, opening all color of rose before her, seemed to her the one enviable path through the world.

In just one day, she realized with vague wonder, her slowly formed theories had been set at naught, her whole philosophy turned upside down. Had these years of protest and rebellion done no more than lead her in a wide circle, past empty gain, and joyless mirth, and the dead sea fruit of riches and idleness, back to her mother's knees again? She had met brilliant women, rich women, courted women— but where among them was one whose face had ever shone as her mother's shone to-day? The overdressed, idle dowagers; the matrons, with their too-gay frocks, their too-full days, their too-rich food; the girls, all crudeness, artifice, all scheming openly for their own advantage,— where among them all was happiness? Where among them was one whom Margaret had heard say—as she had heard her mother say so many, many times,—"Children, this is a happy day,"— "Thank God for another lovely Sunday all together,"—"Isn't it lovely to get up and find the sun shining?"—"Isn't it good to come home hungry to such a nice dinner!"

And what a share of happiness her mother had given the world! How she had planned and worked for them all,—Margaret let her arm fall across the sudden ache in her eyes as she thought of the Christmas mornings, and the stuffed stockings at the fireplace that proved every childish wish remembered, every little hidden hope guessed! Darling Mother—she hadn't had much money for those Christmas stockings, they must have been carefully planned, down to the last candy cane. And how her face would beam, as she sat at the breakfast-table, enjoying her belated coffee, after the cold walk to church, and responding warmly to the onslaught of kisses and bugs that added fresh color to her cold, rosy cheeks! What a mother she was,— Margaret remembered her making them all help her clear up the Christmas disorder of tissue paper and ribbons; then came the inevitable bed making, then tippets and overshoes, for a long walk with Dad. They would come back to find the dining-room warm, the long table set, the house deliciously fragrant from the immense turkey that their mother, a fresh apron over her holiday gown, was basting at the oven. Then came the feast, and then games until twi-light, and more table-setting; and the baby, whoever he was, was tucked away upstairs before tea, and the evening ended with singing, gathered about Mother at the piano.

"How happy we all were!" Margaret said; "and how she worked for us!"

And suddenly theories and speculation ended, and she knew. She knew that faithful, self-forgetting service, and the love that spends itself over and over, only to be renewed again and again, are the secret of happiness. For another world, perhaps, leisure and beauty and lux-ury—but in this one, "Who loses his life shall gain it." Margaret knew now that her mother was not only the truest, the finest, the most generous woman she had ever known, but the happiest as well.

She thought of other women like her mother; she suddenly saw what made their lives beautiful. She could understand now why Emily Porter, her old brave little associate of school-teaching days, was always bright, why Mary Page, plodding home from the long day at the library desk to her little cottage and crippled sister, at night, always made one feel the better and happier for meeting her.

Mrs. Carr-Boldt's days were crowded to the last instant, it was true; but what a farce it was, after all, Margaret said to herself in all honesty, to humor her in her little favorite belief that she was a busy woman! Milliner, manicure, butler, chef, club, card-table, tea table,—these and a thousand things like them filled her day, and they might all be swept away in an hour, and leave no one the worse. Suppose her own summons came; there would be a little flurry throughout the great establishment, legal matters to settle, notes of thanks to be written for flowers. Margaret could imagine Victoria and Harriet, awed but otherwise unaffected, home from school in midweek, and to be sent back before the next Monday. Their lives would go on unchanged, their mother had never buttered bread for them, never schemed for their boots and hats, never watched their work and play, and called them to her knees for praise and blame. Mr. Carr-Boldt would have his club, his business, his yacht, his motor-cars,—he was well accustomed to living in cheerful independence of family claims.

But life without Mother—! In a sick moment of revelation, Margaret saw it. She saw them gathering in the horrible emptiness and silence of the house Mother had kept so warm and bright, she saw her father's stooped shoulders and trembling hands, she saw Julie and Beck, red eyed, white-cheeked, in fresh black,—she seemed to hear the low-toned voices that would break over and over again so cruelly into sobs. What could they do—who could take up the work she laid down,—who would watch and plan and work for them all, now? Margaret thought of the empty place at the table, of the room that, after all these years, was no longer "Mother's room—"

Oh, no—no—no!—She began to cry bitterly in the dark. No, please God, they would hold her safe with them for many years. Mother should live to see some of the fruits of the long labor of love. She should know that with every fresh step in life, with every deepening experience, her children grew to love her better, turned to her more and more! There would be Christmases as sweet as the old ones, if not so gay; there would come a day—Margaret's whole being thrilled to the thought—when little forms would run ahead of John and herself up the worn path, and when their children would be gathered in Mother's experienced arms! Did life hold a more exquisite moment, she wondered, than that in which she would hear her mother praise them!

All her old castles in the air seemed cheap and tinselled to-night, beside these tender dreams that had their roots in the real truths of life. Travel and position, gowns and motor-cars, yachts and country houses, these things were to be bought in all their perfection by the highest bidder, and always would be. But love and character and service, home and the wonderful charge of little lives,—the "pure religion breathing household laws" that guided and perfected the whole,— these were not to be bought, they were only to be prayed for, worked for, bravely won.

"God has been very good to me," Margaret said to herself very seriously; and in her old childish fashion she made some new resolves. From now on, she thought, with a fervor that made it seem half accomplished, she would be a very different woman. If joy came, she would share it as far as she could; if sorrow, she would show her mother that her daughter was not all unworthy of her. To-morrow, she thought, she would go and see Julie. Dear old Ju, whose heart was so full of the little Margaret! Margaret had a sudden tender memory of the days when Theodore and Duncan and Rob were all babies in turn. Her mother would gather the little daily supply of fresh clothes from bureau and chest every morning, and carry the little bath-tub into the sunny nursery window, and sit there with only a bobbing downy head and waving pink angers visible from the great warm bundle of bath apron.... Ju would be doing that now.

And she had sometimes wished, or half formed the wish, that she and Bruce bad been the only ones—! Yes, came the sudden thought, but it wouldn't have been Bruce and Margaret, after all, it would have been Bruce and Charlie.

Good God! That was what women did, then, when they denied the right of life to the distant, unwanted, possible little person! Calmly, constantly, in all placid philosophy and self-justification, they kept from the world—not only the troublesome new baby, with his tears and his illnesses, his merciless exactions, his endless claim on mind and body and spirit—but perhaps the glowing beauty of a Rebecca, the buoyant indomitable spirit of a Ted, the sturdy charm of a small Robert, whose grip on life, whose energy and ambition were as strong as Margaret's own!

Margaret stirred uneasily, frowned in the dark. It seemed perfectly incredible, it seemed perfectly impossible that if Mother had had only the two—and how many thousands of women didn't have that!—she, Margaret, a pronounced and separate entity, travelled, ambitious, and to be the wife of one of the world's great men, might not have been lying here in the summer night, rich in love and youth and beauty and her dreams!

It was all puzzling, all too big for her to understand. But she could do what Mother did, just take the nearest duty and fulfil it, and sleep well, and rise joyfully to fresh effort.

Margaret felt as if she would never sleep again. The summer night was cool, she was cramped and chilly; but still her thoughts raced on, and she could not shut her eyes. She turned and pressed her face resolutely into the pillow, and with a great sigh renounced the joys and sorrows, the lessons and the awakening that the long day had held.

A second later there was a gentle rustle at the door.

"Mark—" a voice whispered. "Can't you sleep?"

Margaret locked her arms tight about her mother, as the older woman knelt beside her.

"Why, how cold you are, sweetheart!" her mother protested, tucking covers about her. "I thought I heard you sigh! I got up to lock the stairway door; Baby's gotten a trick of walking in his sleep when he's overtired. It's nearly one o'clock, Mark! What have you been doing?"

"Thinking." Margaret put her lips close to her mother's ear. "Mother-" she stammered and stopped. Mrs. Paget kissed her.

"Daddy and I thought so," she said simply; and further announcement was not needed. "My darling little girl!" she added tenderly; and then, after a silence, "He is very fine, Mark, so unaffected, so gentle and nice with the boys. I—I think I'm glad, Mark. I lose my girl but there's no happiness like a happy marriage, dear."

"No, you won't lose me, Mother," Margaret said, clinging very close. "We hadn't much time to talk, but this much we did decide. You see, John—John goes to Germany for a year, next July. So we thought— in June or July, Mother, just as Julie's was! Just a little wedding like Ju's. You see, that's better than interrupting the term, or trying to set- tle down, when we'd have to move in July. And, Mother, I'm going to write Mrs. Carr-Boldt,—she can get a thousand girls to take my place, her niece is dying to do it!—and I'm going to take my old school here for the term. Mr. Forbes spoke to me about it after church this morning; they want me back. I want this year at home; I want to see more of Bruce and Ju, and sort of stand by darling little Beck! But it's for you, most of all, Mother," said Margaret, with difficulty. "I've always loved you, Mother, but you don't know how wonderful I think you are—" She broke off pitifully, "Ah, Mother!"

For her mother's arms had tightened convulsively about her, and the face against her own was wet.

"Are you talking?" said Rebecca, rearing herself up suddenly, with a web of bright hair falling over her shoulder. "You said your prayers on Mark last night—" said she, reproachfully, "come over and say them on me to-night, Mother."

Printed in the United States
44851LVS00005B/15